Regina Silsby's
Phantom Militia

Also by Thomas J. Brodeur

Regina Silsby's Secret War

Regina Silsby's
Phantom Militia

by Thomas J. Brodeur

JOURNEY
FORTH™

Greenville, South Carolina

Library of Congress Cataloging-in-Publication Data

Brodeur, Tom.

Regina Silsby's phantom militia / by Thomas J. Brodeur.

p. cm.

Summary: Soon after Rachel Winslow returns to Boston to search for her soldier brother, Regina Silsby comes to the aid of the Patriot cause, this time with reinforcements.

ISBN 1-59166-385-7 (perfect bound pbk. : alk. paper)

1. Boston (Mass.) — History — Colonial period, ca. 1600-1775 — Juvenile fiction. [1. Boston (Mass.) — History — Colonial period, ca. 1600-1775 — Fiction. 2. Ghosts — Fiction. 3. Disguise — Fiction. 4. Cousins — Fiction. 5. Grandfathers — Fiction. 6. Christian life — Fiction.] I. Title: Phantom militia. II. Title.

PZ7.B786113Rdu 2005

[Fic] — dc22

2005002443

Design by Jamie Miller

Cover illustration by Justin Gerard

Composition by Melissa Matos

© 2005 BJU Press

Greenville, SC 29614

Printed in the United States of America

ISBN 1-59166-385-7

15 14 13 12 11 10 9 8 7 6 5 4 3 2 1

To Rachel
for whom I named my heroine.
In all your way acknowledge Him,
and He shall direct your paths.

Contents

Concord, Lexington, and Boston—1775

CONCORD

LEXINGTON

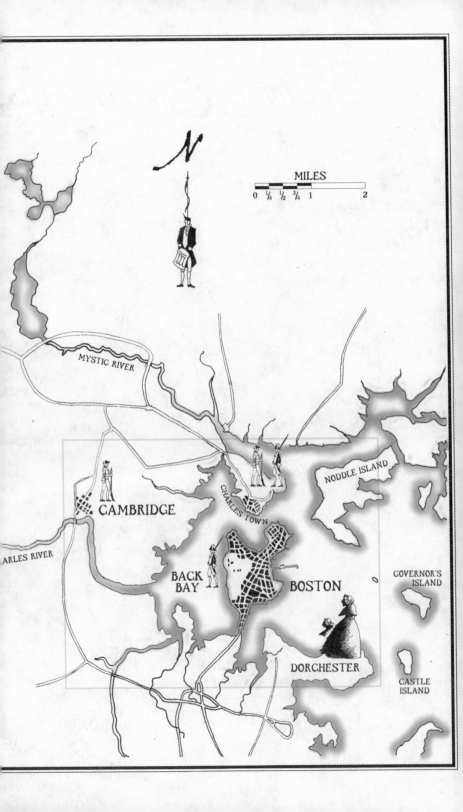

MILES

0 ¼ ½ ¾ 1 2

MYSTIC RIVER

CAMBRIDGE

CHARLES TOWN

NODDLE ISLAND

CHARLES RIVER

BACK BAY

BOSTON

GOVERNOR'S ISLAND

DORCHESTER

CASTLE ISLAND

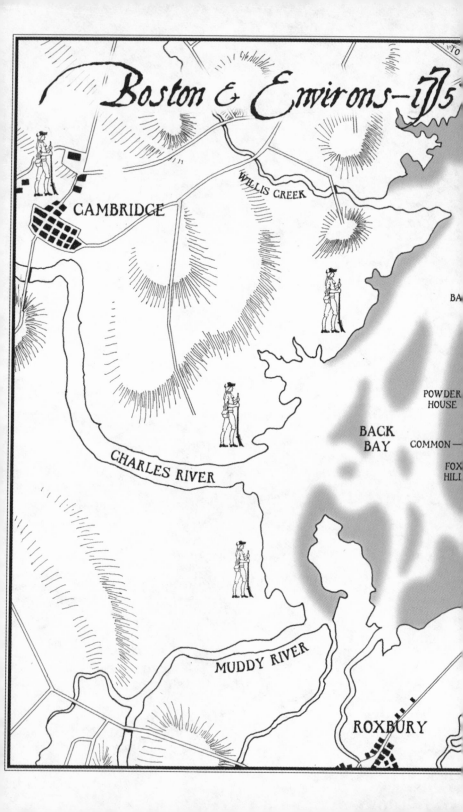

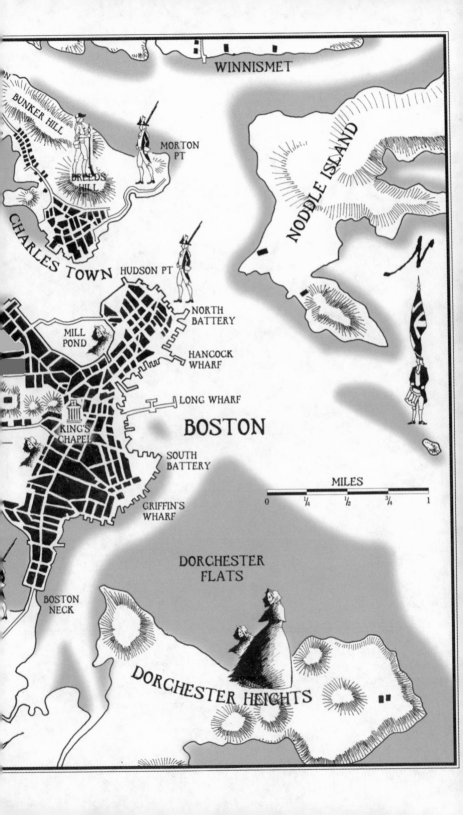

One

An April Morn

Rachel Winslow bolted upright. Was that a musket shot?

She scanned the dark bedchamber. Embers warmed the hearth on the far wall, and aroma of cedar scented the room. Frost etched the window beside the bed. A shaft of moonlight cast luminous squares across her quilt, and rhythmic buzzing sounded from the mound at her side. Cousin Sarah was fast asleep.

"What's the hour?" she wondered. Grandfather kept a timepiece in his waistcoat pocket. Should she cross the chilly floorboards to the corner, where he lay snoring in his bed-roll? She shivered and reached for the mug of sassafras tea on the nightstand. Long ago the drink had gone cold, but still she drained it to the dregs.

Another shot shattered the stillness. Across the street a church bell clanged.

"Sarah, wake up," she said, prodding her cousin. "I heard gunshots, and now the belfry is tolling."

" 'Tis the dead of night," Sarah said.

Grandfather tugged on his boots.

"You two stay abed," he said. "We're strangers in this town, and I'll not have you roaming about."

"Perhaps there is a fire," Rachel said. Drums beat a call to arms.

"I think not, lass."

After throwing on his cloak, he slipped through the door and latched it shut. Rachel sprang from the bed. She lit a candle and laced on her petticoats.

"Did you not hear?" Sarah said. "We're to stay put."

"I wish to learn what's the fuss."

"And you'll be wanting company, I suppose."

"Are you not curious?"

Sarah cast off the quilt and swung her feet to the floor. Blonde hair fell in tangles about her cheeks. She yawned, stretched, and pulled her green paisley gown over her camisole and bloomers.

"You'll want to wear your flannels," Rachel said while gathering her dark tresses into a bun.

"We shan't be more than a minute."

Into the corridor they wandered and down the stairs to the front hall.

"Mind your step, lasses," said the innkeeper. He stood at the rear entry holding aloft a candelabrum. Servants and stable hands trundled casks through the open doorway.

"Everything into the barn," he said. "Rum, hard cider, everything. And touch not a drop, or I'll have your hides off of you. Mrs. Wright, hurry on."

The fat woman emerged from the larder tugging sacks stuffed to bursting. Her face was flushed and sweaty.

"Lasses," she said, "take these to the hayloft, quick now."

"What's happened?" Rachel said.

"Don't waste time chattering, dear. Off with you."

"Aye, madame."

Across the stable yard the girls dragged the duffels.

"How are we going to lift these to the loft?" Sarah said. "They're so heavy."

"You, boy," Rachel said to a stable hand, "could you lend a hand, please? The missus wants these in the loft."

"Right away, miss."

He hauled away the sacks, and the girls pushed through a picket gate to the road. Torches brightened a tumult of townsmen, wagons, and horses. Through the din of shouted orders and bellowing animals clattered the church bell, and from the village green came a steady thump of drums. Horses crowded the tavern's hitching rails, their booted riders adjusting saddlestraps. Cellar doors flung open. On every step appeared rifles and cartridge pouches. Citizens scooped them up as quickly as they were laid out.

At the meetinghouse a line of farmers and journeymen lugged kegs to a hay wagon.

"Careful with those," said the wagon master. "You'll blow us all to bits."

"That's the last of it," said a tailored gentleman in a white wig. "You know where to take them?"

"Aye, into the forests beyond the north bridge. Ho, lads, spread that hay over them well."

Women shoveled their gardens and pitched canvas satchels into the holes. A lady clad in a linen nightshirt, her gray hair billowing down her back and her bare feet caked with mud, dumped a silver tea service into a soap barrel.

"Good sir," Rachel said to a passing horseman, "what's the news?"

"The regulars are out," he said, "a thousand strong. They're coming by way of the Boston road."

"For what purpose?"

"To arrest Hancock and Adams at Lexington, I'm told, and to take the munitions and stores here at Concord. Fret not, lass, they shall miss their aim. But if you've anything of value, you must hide it straightaway."

"How thrilling," Sarah said. "The Boston redcoats come this way, Rachel. Is it not grand?"

"Are you mad? Why should that please you?"

"Don't you see? We expected to reach Boston on the morrow, and tonight it seems that Boston is coming to us. Do you suppose the ghost will follow after them?"

"What ghost?"

"Regina Silsby, of course."

"Good heavens, Sarah. You mustn't speak of her."

"Why not? Every circuit rider out of New England talked endlessly about her. You heard their stories of Regina Silsby

4

dashing all about, terrifying the king's soldiers and running ships aground, then vanishing away before anyone could catch her. They said she haunts the King's Chapel, where she's buried. Oh, it makes me shudder. Are our Boston lodgings near her grave?"

"Do you hope to see her?"

"Of course."

"Perhaps we should make camp in the cemetery and watch for her there. Really, Sarah, you must stop this nonsense. Very few people saw her, and those who did wished they hadn't."

" 'Tisn't fair, Rachel, you dwelling in Boston with Regina Silsby's ghost, while I suffered an endless string of tutors in Philadelphia. There wasn't a handsome one among them."

"Boston was hardly exciting."

"How can you say that, with the Massacre and the Tea Party and Regina Silsby haunting the streets? Why do you think I wished to journey along with you?"

"To help bring my brother out of Boston, or so I supposed."

"And to see the ghost."

"Sarah, you're daft. Come along, we must hide our effects before the soldiers arrive."

They darted through the tavern entry to the stair.

"I do hope they shall show us a good parade," Sarah said.

"If you must wag your tongue, pray that nothing awful happens."

Sarah halted, clamped shut her eyes and pressed her hands together.

"Gracious God," she said, "in whose good mercies are our sustenance and our life, grant Thou that we may—"

"For goodness' sake, Sarah, can you not walk and pray at the same time?"

"Rachel Winslow, you are positively irreverent."

"Get up here at once. Put this in your pocket."

She handed Sarah one of Grandfather's pistols.

"Take the bullet molds," she said, "and the powder horns. I'll keep the other two, and the flints and musket balls. Here is Grandfather's spyglass."

Sarah peeled back her skirt and tied her pocket apron to her waist.

"A fine pistol, this," she said, squinting along its barrel. "French, is it?"

"I'm not certain."

"*Le Guardienne*," she read from the firelock's engraving. "Rifled too. Very fine, indeed."

She shoved the gun into a hip pouch, and draped the powder horns about her waist. Rachel laced on her riding boots. The door opened.

"We've a regiment of redcoats marching on Concord," Grandfather said. "What are you two about?"

"Hiding what we can," Rachel said. "They may search the house, but they shan't search our persons."

"Where are my pistols?"

"In our pockets. I have your spyglass as well."

"Don't stuff yourselves too much, or you'll be fatter than the innkeeper's wife. Come, let's have your kits. I'll take them to the attic with my saddlebag."

They handed him their satchels. After he disappeared, Rachel pressed her nose to the window.

"I can't see through this ice," she said, and heaved open the sash. Dawn colored the eastern sky. Morning mist veiled the hillocks of verdant green. Stone walls and budding trees separated fields wet with dew. Beyond the forests tumbled a river swollen by spring rains.

"Sarah, listen."

Fifes trilled through the rush of cascading water and clanging bells.

"They're playing 'Yankee Doodle,' " Sarah said. "Show of good faith, I'll wager."

"While coming to steal Concord's stores? Perhaps they would pilfer the tune as well."

"You're such a doomsayer."

"Have you already forgotten? Until last year I dwelt in Boston. I've had more than my fill of redcoats.

"Rachel, don't lean through the window like that. You'll fall on your head."

"Look, Sarah, yonder they come."

Scarlet horsemen jostled over a rise, their tasseled shoulders glinting in the first rays of sunlight. Regimental flags flapped in their wake, and columns of crimson soldiers trudged after them. Every man's breeches were black to the hip with mud.

"They look as though they marched through a swamp," Sarah said. "How disappointing."

At the head of the army plodded a fat colonel on a tired mount. Sullen inhabitants stared from windows and doorways as he halted the parade at the meetinghouse.

"Maj. Cauldon," he said, "you will issue the orders, please."

"Aye, sir," said a mounted officer at his flank. "Grenadiers, disperse. Search every house; destroy all contraband. Capt. Laurie, you'll post your companies at the north bridge, and Capt. Pole, you may secure the south crossing."

"Aye, sir."

Officers exchanged salutes, and scarlet ranks spread through the village.

"Innkeeper," said the colonel, reining his horse toward the tavern, "what have you for breakfast? I and my men have been a'march all night."

Soldiers battered down doors and smashed windows. The troops pillaged whatever fancied them—timepieces, jewelry, silver, pewter, copper.

"Come inside, Rachel, and close that window," Sarah said. "They shall see you."

"Not just yet."

"Maj. Cauldon, sir," said a sergeant, "we found three unmounted field cannon in the livery, and their carriages. There's five barrels of musket balls in the town house."

"Any gunpowder?"

"None, sir. I expect most everything's been moved during the night."

"Cursed, scheming scoundrels. Very well, Sergeant, spike the guns, fire the town house."

"Aye, sir."

"Col. Smith, sir," Cauldon said, "I request permission to lead a detachment of light infantry beyond the town."

"Will you not join me first for a bit of breakfast, Major?"

8

"I think some haste would be in order, sir. Whatever stores have been removed may not be sufficiently hidden."

"Very well, if you insist. Make certain you destroy the bridge after you've done with it."

"Thank you, sir."

Black smoke and flame billowed from the town house.

"Rachel, do come inside," Sarah said. "You shall get us both into trouble."

"Hush. How can I hear what is said with you jabbering like that?"

A shot echoed beyond the woods. Rippling volleys followed.

"Mercy," Sarah said, "is that gunfire?"

She squeezed into the window beside her cousin.

"Bother," she said. "The fighting's past the trees. Why did they choose to have their battle there?"

A thunderclap rebounded from the river. The staccato of answering shots thickened into a roar. Smoke plumed through the forest and drifted across the village green. From the haze ran a lone soldier.

"Col. Smith, sir," he said, saluting. "There's rebel minute-men—hundreds of them—attacking us at the north bridge. Capt. Laurie requests immediate assistance."

"Madness," Smith said through a mouthful of mutton. " 'Tis farmers we're up against, not the French. Surely the captain is capable of handling these poltroons."

"They fear us not, sir. We are badly outnumbered."

"Preposterous. A good show of force will hurl them into the hills."

"The provincials are well hidden behind fences and trees, sir. Our volleys affected them not at all."

"Did I ask your opinion, private? Report back to the captain and tell him I said to be about his business. Badly outnumbered, indeed."

"Sarah, look there," Rachel said, pointing. A torrent of scarlet troops tumbled from the smoke. Hats were missing, muskets gone, tunics torn, breeches bloodied, flags and drums peppered with holes. Terror marred every face. The stricken soldiers poured into the village.

"Rally," officers shouted, swatting men with the flats of their swords. "Reform your ranks."

Smith bolted from his table, his napkin still tucked to his chin.

"Return to your ranks," he yelled. "Form up, I say."

Sergeants swung fists and cudgels, even grabbed fleeing soldiers by their collars. In the forest appeared ragged clusters of riflemen. They wore farmers' frocks, town coats, buckskins. Some stood in their shirtsleeves; many were barefooted.

"Look, Rachel," Sarah said, pointing. "Yonder are the patriots. Hooray!"

Flashes brightened the trees. Smith pitched forward and lay in the grass.

"Sergeant," Cauldon yelled, "rig a stretcher at once. Carry the colonel back to Lexington. Captains, I shall assume command in the colonel's absence."

"Major, there's thousands of them," said a battered officer. "Every rock and tree harbors a rifle. We tried to hold the bridge, but . . ."

"Get your men to the rear, Captain," Cauldon said. "Edwards, send a scout to the south crossing and summon Capt. Pole back at once. We must evacuate Concord, now. Each captain will be responsible for his own company. Fall back to Lexington and rally at the common, understood? Lord Percy shall meet us there with a relief column."

"But sir," said a lieutenant. "The field guns—the rebels will take them back from us."

"You spiked the touchholes, did you not? Forget them. Fire as many houses and fields as you can and fall back. I shall remain to bring up the rear."

Drums beat the signal to withdraw. Already the towns-folk were retrieving flour casks from the river and dragging the field guns back to the livery. Soldiers hurled torches into homes and barns, but inhabitants quickly doused the flames. Shots flashed from open windows.

"Hurry on, you louts," Cauldon said, his horse engulfed in the flood of swirling scarlet. "Get along, quick march."

Minutemen spilled into the town.

"Move your legs," Cauldon said as bullets whistled past him, "or your carcasses will feed the buzzards tonight."

He cantered among the fleeing ranks, urging the men onto the highway, rounding up the laggards. From every tree, wall, and field came incessant firing. Soldiers collapsed in the grass and on the lanes.

"Look, Rachel," Sarah said, bouncing up and down, "the patriots have put them to flight."

A clapboard near her head splintered. She yelped and retreated behind the bed. The door banged open.

"Rachel, away from that window," Grandfather said. "Are you mad?"

"We're being shot at," Sarah said.

"We must get to Boston," he said, "before that redcoat army reaches the city."

"But where is Regina Silsby?" Sarah said. "Why has she not come?"

"Time enough to fret about her later, child. We'll travel the north country to Charlestown and ferry across the harbor from there. Sarah, get you downstairs to the innkeeper and order our horses saddled."

"I shall be killed."

"The battle's already moved beyond the town, lass. Hurry on; we've no time to lose."

"But . . ."

"Go, child, now."

"Aye, sir." She bustled from the chamber.

"Rachel," he said, "this little fracas today complicates our chore a good bit. You mustn't be seen in Boston's streets. If someone should recognize you—"

"We can't have Sarah running all our errands."

"Come nightfall," he said, "I'll go to Josiah Sinquin's shop and fetch Robert out. We'll leave Boston by the same route we came."

"I am quicker than you," she said. "Perhaps I should go."

"The streets won't be safe."

"I've done it before."

"As Regina Silsby, aye," he said. "There wasn't a man sober or drunk who dared go near you as the ghost."

"Should I disguise myself as before? It is easily done."

"Mercy, child. 'Twas only last year you nearly got yourself hanged for your escapades. Are you so eager to start them again?"

"How difficult can it be? I shall fetch Robert out of Sinquin's shop and return before you've missed me. If anyone sees us, I shall scare him to death."

Grandfather sighed.

"There's no denying you're nimbler than I," he said. "And you're certainly a formidable phantom. Very well then, I suppose you'll be needing this."

He dug into his saddlebag and extracted a leather mask.

"I wore this," he said, "when I followed after you before."

From her cape pocket she produced her own mask and said, "I, too, have come prepared."

"Bless my soul, child."

He inspected the leather. Its tattered skin, blackened eye-holes, and gnarled mouth were uglier than a rotted corpse.

"Is this the same face you wore before?" he said.

"The very one. Regina Silsby has returned to Boston."

"Well," he said, "your cousin Sarah wishes to see the ghost. Perhaps she'll get her chance."

Two

❧

Again the Ghost

Stars dusted the night sky, and distant surf thundered on a sea breeze stirring the elms. Rachel crouched in the garden hedge behind the Hound's Tooth Tavern. Weeks had been wasted seeking a boatman bold enough to smuggle her, Sarah, and Grandfather across the Charles River to Boston. The bloodshed at Lexington and Concord had panicked the entire British garrison, and they were letting no one enter the city.

In the shadows she slipped on Regina Silsby's mask and laced it behind her head. Her bald skull she covered with the mangled hairpiece that had once been her father's wig. Black gloves stretched to her elbows, with strips of white linen sewn on them to resemble bones. Beneath her dress she wore a pair of Grandfather's breeches—the better to run with—and her riding boots were tightly laced from ankle to knee. A hooded cloak completed her disguise.

At a rain barrel she paused to inspect her reflection. Decayed flesh collapsed around two sinkholes harboring wild eyes. A mutilated mass of lips and teeth oozed like festering rot. Surrounding the gore was an explosion of ashen hair. She smiled, and the face contorted into a grimace.

"Regina Silsby, you are uglier than ever," she said. With gloved fingers she tousled her tresses until they were as messy as humanly possible. She then pushed through the hedge, climbed the picket fence, and dropped to the cobbles beyond.

"Grant me favor, Lord," she said. "Let this be a quick trip."

Shop windows facing the street were shuttered, and their signboards gone. Musketed sentries paced the lanes. Despite the darkness she was glad to tread the familiar paths of home. Certainly Philadelphia enjoyed many advantages over Boston, with its straight boulevards and numbered avenues, where carriages passed three and four abreast, and lanterns brightened every street corner. Boston was a tangle of narrow, twisting lanes that ended abruptly and changed their names at whim. Orange Street became Newbury at the Liberty Tree, then called itself Marlbrough, and finally ended as Cornhill. Dock Square was hardly more than a mangled meeting of seven roads. Oliver Street transformed itself into Kirby until crossing King, where it changed to Merchant's Row. South Street was east; North Square was not square; Water Street was far from water; Cow Lane had no cows. Only Short Street was rightly named, and it was not easily found. For visitors Boston was miserable, but for phantoms it was perfect.

She melted into a niche as two chattering tradesmen ambled by.

"Stay away," said a gaunt man on a doorstep. "There's a pox upon this dwelling. Already two children are dead from it, and the missus won't be far behind. Stay away."

Black flags draped the entry. The tradesmen darted to the far side of the street and hurried by, cupping hands to their faces. Rachel slipped through an alley to the neighboring lane. Before she had reached the next crossroads, she saw more black flags.

Soldiers crowded the waterfront. In and out of entries they bustled, stacking weapons, counting cartridges, stuffing rucksacks. Conversations were whispered, orders hushed. She slunk from shadow to shadow until a carriage lumbered to a halt in front of her, forcing her beneath the bricked steps of a tavern. Cats screeched as she squeezed into the cramped space. The tavern entry opened, and a shaft of light fell across the cobbles.

"Ah, Maj. Cauldon, there you are," said a voice from the stone above her. "What's the word?"

"Gen. Gage has agreed to my plan," said the major. His boot splashed water in Rachel's face as he stepped from the carriage. "We're to post six companies and field artillery on the Charlestown heights by Sunday night. The orders will be issued Saturday."

"About time. How did you convince him?"

"It was not easy. Has the innkeeper any brandy? We must celebrate."

"Grog and flip is all he's got."

"Stupid oaf."

They retreated into the tavern, and the door banged shut. Rachel wriggled from her shelter. She scooted between the carriage wheels, emerging on the far side of the coach. The driver was already dozing. She patted the horses while slipping by them.

So close was her former home that she decided to venture past it. Tents surrounded the dwelling with trails crisscrossing the trampled lawns and flowerbeds. All the garden trees and shrubs were gone. Picket fences had been torn down, window shutters stripped away. Broken glass marked her bedchamber. The neighbors' houses had vanished, probably to fuel cooking fires. Before long her own dwelling might disappear as well.

Her heart sank, but with work to be done she could not wallow in sorrow. Down the lane she drifted, avoiding lanterns and dissolving into crevices when strangers approached. Several townsmen strolled within arm's reach of her, unaware that a bony claw could have grabbed at them from the shadows. After they had passed, she crept on, until at last she faced the shop of Josiah Sinquin, the jeweler.

The signboard was missing, and the bay windows were black. Robert usually slept in a back room with the window ajar. She followed a side alley to the building's rear and found the pane as she expected. Carefully she lifted the sash and eased through the opening. Floorboards creaked beneath her boots. With her back pressed to the wall, she let her eyes adjust to the darkness. The chamber was crammed with crates and casks. There was no bed, no sound of a slumbering inhabitant. Slowly she crossed the room and lifted the door latch. Odors of animal fat and tallow stung her nostrils. A narrow passage led to the shop, where vats crusted with wax clogged the floor. Hanging from the ceiling were hundreds of candlesticks. Her trepidation mounted. This was not a jeweler's shop.

"Who's there?" said a voice. She shrank into the shadows. On a cot by the bay window sat a boy silhouetted in moonlight.

"I . . . I know you're there," he said, his voice trembling. "Show yourself."

She stood motionless, hoping he would mistake her for clutter.

"Mr. Fulkes, is that you?" he said. "Are you wanting something?"

He eased from the cot and groped toward the workbench. Iron utensils clattered to the floor.

"Quiet, boy," said a gravelly voice overhead. "You should be abed."

"Mr. Fulkes, come quickly. Someone's in the shop."

"Liar. You're stealing the cider again. Insolent pup."

"Sir, there's a thief here, I'm certain. Please come at once."

"A thief, is it? Very well, I shall deal with him directly. And if you're lying, boy, I shall have your hide off of you."

Candlelight shimmered on a narrow stair. Down the planks wobbled an old man, his bare legs protruding beneath his nightshirt. In one hand he clutched a lighted taper, in the other a pistol. His hair was tousled, his cheeks unshaved, and with blinking eyes he surveyed the chamber. When his gaze met Rachel's, he gasped and toppled backward.

"Saints alive," he said. " 'Tis the King's Chapel ghost."

She seized a tin mold and hurled it at him. With a yelp he dropped the candle, plunging the shop into blackness. A fireball flashed and thunder boomed. The shot ricocheted off the hearth and shattered a window. Shrieks filled the chamber. Outside a dog barked. Boots tramped the cobbles.

Rachel leapt toward the bay window and shoved aside the screaming boy. She braced her arms over her head and lunged through the pane. In a shower of shattering glass she slammed a pillar that collapsed with her to the pavement. It was the night watchman. She snarled into his disbelieving face.

Behind her the shop entry flung open.

"Alarm!" yelled the shopkeeper, dashing by her without seeing her. He hammered doors across the lane. The boy ran after him ringing a hand bell.

"Help, help!" he shouted. "The witch's ghost assaulted us."

Rachel wrestled the watchman for his pistol. Her claws lacerated his arm, and her teeth ripped into his wrist. He howled.

"Mr. Fulkes, look there," said the boy. "She's possessed that fellow."

The watchman's gun erupted. She tore it from his grasp, battered his brow, and sprang for the shadows. Soldiers and citizens stampeded toward the shop.

"What's all the shouting?" said a lieutenant.

"Regina Silsby," said the shopkeeper. "She attacked us."

"You don't mean the ghost."

"A filthy corpse she is," said the boy. "Her face is rotted away, and her arms are bones. Mr. Fulkes shot her, but it harmed her not at all."

"Night Watch, what say you? Did you see her?"

The watchman groaned.

"Speak, man," said the lieutenant, shaking him. "What happened?"

"A demon," said the watchman, "with claws sharp as knives. And fangs . . . like a wolf's."

" 'Twas Regina Silsby that assailed him," said the boy. "I saw her. She would carry him to the grave."

Torches and lanterns brightened the lane. Overhead windows banged open. The dreaded name passed from house to house.

"Form a search party," said the lieutenant. "Sergeant, rouse the company. She can't have gone far."

"Aye, sir."

Rachel fled through tangled alleys. All around her townsmen shouted Regina Silsby's name. Drums rapped alarm.

"She's bound for her grave at King's Chapel," someone said. "Fetch the torches there."

She sighed her relief. The cemetery was opposite her intended route. Cobbles beneath her feet trembled as crowds surged toward the church. Before she could peel off her disguise, a soldier spied her.

"There she is," he said to his comrades. Instead of pursuing her, they fled.

"Get you after her," said an officer, beating them with a riding crop. "Fix bayonets and bring her here."

The troops clamped steel pikes to their muskets. She dashed around a corner and dove under a stone step. They ran past, followed by the officer. As their footsteps faded, she emerged and doubled back. Behind a clapboard house she climbed a fence and tumbled into a pigsty. The slumbering hogs ignored her, until she stepped on a curled tail.

Loud squeals triggered an eruption of frantic yelping. Boots thumped toward her.

"Here," the officer said, his sword flashing beyond the fence. Muskets battered apart the planks. A soldier struggled through the hole and was trampled by fleeing swine. Rachel vaulted the fence opposite.

"Hold there," said a man at the house's back entry. "Who's stealing my pigs?"

"Out of my way," the officer said. With his sword hilt he punched the man's face. A woman in an upper window screamed.

"On your feet, you louts," the officer told his men. "Don't lose her."

Rachel scampered across the next street. Hounds began to bay. She halted, terrified. Was someone tracking her with dogs? They would follow her straight to her bed. She had to mask her scent, but there were no trees to shinny, no rooftops low enough to climb.

"Oh, Lord, what shall I do?" she said, searching the surrounding buildings. Before her stood a carriage house with a barn beside it. Agitated horses jostled within.

"Hah!" she said and raced for the stable. Inside were eight steeds. Their bridles and livery belonged to British cavalry. She unlatched the stalls and prodded the animals toward the entry. Lacking time to properly saddle a mount, she seized the largest stallion's mane and swung herself onto his bare back. A swat to his rump sent him leaping through the barn door. The other horses stampeded after him. Soldiers approaching the entry scattered screaming.

With her legs she gripped the horse's flanks, but no matter how she tore his mane the stallion refused to be steered. Helplessly she careened through the streets with seven lathered steeds thundering after her. Every bounce of the animal's body sent her sliding farther down his back. Before long she would plunge to the pavement, and the trailing horses would trample her to a pulp.

A carriage crossed her path. The stallion swerved past it while the driver wrestled his rearing charges. Sentries flung themselves into doorways. One fellow splashed into a watering trough. Benches and barrels overturned. Two men standing on a tavern step shrieked in terror.

"The ghost," they said. "Regina Silsby."

Down a narrow lane the horses lunged, hooves battering the cobbles. Rachel bumped along the stallion's back, her fingers gripping his mane, her belly banging his spine. Through the steed's tossing hair she spied a coach clopping toward her. Already the driver was tightening his reins, expecting a collision. The street was too narrow for safe passage. She clamped shut her eyes.

Abruptly her stallion halted. She skidded up his back and over his neck, clutching his throat to keep from toppling. The other horses paused behind him, nostrils flared and huffing. Amazed, she sat up and stared at the carriage's driver, who gaped at her.

"Good evening," she said, choking back her voice. The words rumbled from her throat like the croak of a hoarse toad.

"Good evening to you," he said, trembling.

She slid from the horse's back, and her wobbly legs carried her past the coach. Two tailored gentlemen and their bejeweled ladies stared at her through the carriage windows. She shared a gaze with one woman, who promptly fainted.

Beyond the coach she forced her legs to run. At the first crossroads she dove into a dark corner. There she caught her breath and tried to calm her palpitating heart. Men carrying torches hurried by her.

"Regina Silsby's up from her grave," they said. "Beware the ghost."

Other voices shouted the news in neighboring lanes. She tugged off her wig, gloves, and mask and stuffed them under her skirt. After smoothing her hair, she emerged from the shadows.

Familiar houses lined the curb. The horse had not carried her too far off course. She scurried the lanes, telling everyone she passed, "Regina Silsby's arisen. Beware."

"Get you home, girl, at once."

"Aye, straightaway. Pray she doesn't put a curse on all of us."

Soon she was pushing through the Hound's Tooth gate and crossing the stable yard. In the tavern windows she saw soldiers guzzling beer, singing, and playing at gambols and cards. Beneath the huge elm in the garden she scanned the roof for her gabled window. Ash from Grandfather's pipe glowed in the dark opening.

She whistled a whippoorwill's cry. A similar chirp trilled from the window, and a plank came spinning down the tree on a rope.

"Sit on the board, lass," Grandfather said. She tucked the plank between her legs and was hoisted upward. No sooner had the tree's canopy swallowed her than a patrol of soldiers tramped beneath.

"Search everything," the sergeant said. His men probed the bushes, the larder, and the stable while Rachel dangled mutely above them.

"Nothing, sir," they said.

"I'm sure I saw her come through here."

"There's no one about, sir. We've looked everywhere."

"Very well, move onto the next house."

"Sir, you don't suppose she's . . . disappeared."

"Imbecile. 'Tis flesh and blood we're hunting, not a spirit. Move along."

The soldiers departed, and the plank resumed its jerking ascent.

"Grab the sill, lass," Grandfather said when she was level with the window. He seized her wrist and hauled her through the opening.

"Well enough," he said. "You're safe now."

"Thank God."

She threw her arms around his neck and heaved a grateful sigh.

"There, there, child," he said, patting her back. "Bit of a fright you've had, I'd say."

"A bit."

"Somebody saw you?"

"A tallow merchant. He shouted alarm."

She released him and examined the rope. It threaded a pulley lashed to the tree and was cleated to a corner post of the bed. Sarah lay beneath the sheets, snoring.

Three

Tidings

"This bosun's chair may serve us later," Grandfather said, coiling the rope around the plank. With his cane he hung it on a tree limb just outside the window.

"Did you rig it yourself?" Rachel said.

"Aye, while you were out. Found the tackle in the attic yonder, and the board's from the barn. Where's Robert?"

"Gone," she said. "A tallow merchant has set up shop in Sinquin's stead. Quite a fright I gave him."

"Did he recognize you?"

"As Regina Silsby, aye. He cried alarm. Soldiers are searching the streets now."

"Bad luck," he said, "and we've more to trouble us."

"How so?"

"I ventured into the taproom for a dram of conversation. Sarah helped the mistress serve, and between us we collected a trunk load of tidings. Word is that no one may leave Boston without a military pass signed by one Maj. Small. He's to be found at the Province House."

"You mean we're trapped here?"

"We may find a boat along the wharves," he said, "and steal across the harbor by night just as we came in. There's rebel militia camped about Boston from Dorchester to Chelsea, thousands of them. I'm told that General Gage has offered pardon to all who will lay down their arms."

"Has anyone done so?"

"Not thus far. Some pickets are less than a musket shot from the town gate."

"What are you two babbling about?" Sarah said. She sat up, stretched, and scratched her head. Feathers dusted her long hair.

"Rachel, there you are," she said. "What has kept you out so long?"

"I . . . tarried with several army officers," she said. "Aye, that's where I was. They took me all across town."

"You went without me?"

"I'm sorry, Sarah. We were off and about before I was able to think of it."

"How could you leave me to pass the night in a kitchen?"

"It really was not pleasant. We went looking for Robert."

"If that be so, where is he?"

"Nowhere to be found, I'm afraid. What's worse, we cannot leave the city."

"That I know already."

"Not all the news is bad," Grandfather said. "Fort Ticonderoga's fallen to the rebels."

"Is it close by?" Rachel said.

"Lake Champlain, northwest of here," he said. "The rebels took her without a shot. They've captured upwards of sixty cannon, and the fear among the redcoats is that those guns will be brought against Boston."

"To bombard the city?"

"Not the town, but the British fleet in the harbor. With rebel cannon on the hills, the fleet will have to evacuate. And if they go, they must take the British garrison with them."

"You mean the British would be forced to abandon Boston?" Rachel said.

"Precisely."

"Is it not wonderful?" Sarah said. "A patriot victory."

"Unless," Grandfather said, "the British occupy the heights first. Then the problem's reversed. 'Twill be the British bombarding the rebel militias, and the rebels will do the evacuating."

"And leave the entire countryside in British hands," Rachel said.

"Whoever occupies the heights," Grandfather said, "controls the land. Seems to me, somebody should be moving to fortify the hills."

"Someone is," Rachel said with a groan. "Orders will be issued Saturday to occupy the heights above Charlestown."

"Bunker's Hill?" he said.

"Artillery's to be in place Sunday."

"Who told you this?"

"The officers . . . were discussing it," she said. "By next week the far shores could be under the British flag. We won't escape Boston by land or sea."

"Sunday, is it?" Grandfather said, stroking his chin. "Five days hence."

"It may be time enough to find Robert."

"Not so much as you think, lass. Today's already spent. Saturday and Sunday may be lost as well, since the troops will be taking up their positions on those days. That leaves tomorrow and Friday. If we haven't left by dawn Saturday, we may not be leaving at all."

"Two days," Rachel said.

"There's no telling where your brother might be, child. Best we get ourselves out while we're able."

"We cannot leave without Robert," she said.

"We may be lucky to escape with our own skins."

"I promised Mother I'd return with him."

"And I promised her I'd return with you. Rachel, we're in the middle of a war. Sometimes 'tis best to cut your losses and run."

"Robert is not a loss, Grandfather; he's my brother—and your grandson."

"Listen to me, lass. Robert's well on his way to manhood and able to look after himself. He's in the Lord's hands, not yours. You would do well to remember that. Some troubles are God's to fret about, not ours."

"We cannot go without him," she said, crossing her arms. Grandfather sighed. He leaned on the windowpane and gazed into the courtyard below.

"I suppose," he said, puffing his pipe, "our problem might be solved if the rebels were to occupy Bunker's Hill first."

"How is that possible?" Rachel said.

"We might find a way to alert them to the redcoats' plan."

"You have an idea?"

"I heard some names bandied about," he said. "William Prescott is a colonel of militia in Cambridge. There's also a Gen. Putnam—'Old Put,' the innkeeper called him."

"We must get ourselves to Cambridge straightaway," Rachel said.

"Hold on, lass. Think carefully what you're about. You're talking sedition, treason, aiding enemies of the crown. If caught, you'll hang for a spy."

"What would you do, Grandfather?"

"Haint my choice to make. My life's done. 'Tis your future—and Sarah's—we're gambling. Oppressive the king may be, but to cast your lot with the rebels may be trading one tyrant for a thousand worse ones. You may even find yourself fighting against God, instead of with Him."

"I say we go to Cambridge at once," Sarah said.

Rachel pondered the implications. Grandfather would not tell her how to choose, but he would support the choice she made. What did Holy Scripture say? Absalom had rebelled against his father King David and had been smitten of God for it. Moses had opposed Egypt's pharaoh and had liberated the Israelites. Which was the proper course, to support the English king or resist him?

And what of the rebels? Were they traitorous subjects or oppressed slaves? Would God fight for His chosen people and destroy the British pharaoh's army? At Lexington and Concord a band of farmers had struck the redcoats a resounding blow, just as Joshua had routed the Canaanites at Jericho. If the rebels did manage to throw off their British yoke, what sort of fetter would they fashion to replace it? Would their government be a pinnacle of light and liberty, or a cave of deep, unending darkness? Only one person knew.

"Let us pray on this," she said.

"Pray?" Sarah said. "Do you mean now?"

"Shall we wait until the Sabbath? Really, Sarah, if you cannot pray in time of need, when can you? God will never answer us if we do not entreat Him."

"And do you really expect to hear from Him? He never answers me."

"You don't hear Him with your ears, Sarah. He stirs your spirit, like a breeze. All you need do is sit quietly and listen for Him."

"How long?"

"As long as needed."

"You mean for me to sit here until God stirs my spirit? I've been blustering about the taproom all evening. I want to sleep."

"We shan't do all our listening at once. Prayers are like musket balls. You fire one off, reload, and follow it with another. After shooting a bagful, you put the gun away and go about your business and pick it up again on the morrow and shoot again."

"Or I suppose you can shoot all day long while you're busy about your chores."

"Until one of your shots strikes true. In the end you find all of them do."

"How funny, Rachel. I can just see you wandering about your house shooting holes in all the walls."

"The more holes, the better the breezes blow."

"Especially in winter."

They laughed.

"Teach me to pray this way," Sarah said.

"Very well."

She took Sarah's hand.

"You don't sign the cross on yourself?" Sarah said.

"Usually not."

"Do you fold your hands?"

"We're speaking to God, Sarah, not casting a spell. There's no formula to it. Prayers work because God hears."

"Let's get to praying, then," Grandfather said, "and stop all this jabbering about it."

He gripped the girls' hands, and together they bowed their heads.

"Dearest Father in heaven," Rachel said, "how glad I am that You are sovereign. Already You know this war's outcome and its purpose for being. We are sinners lost in darkness. We cannot even see the morrow, but You see everything. I pray You will reveal Your thoughts to us. Is America to be liberated, or is she a rebellious child in need of a whipping? Show us what You are about in this conflict, Lord. Show us what we are to do in it. We've a puzzle before us just now. Do we go to Cambridge and alert the rebels, or do we remain in Boston and hold our tongues? Do we look for Robert, or go home? Please tell us."

Scattered thoughts spilled through her mind. To do nothing was to permit a British success. To act might alter the course of the conflict but might also afflict her with much trouble. She pondered her grandfather's youth. What tales he told of audacious raids against pirates, of perilous rescues and fearful forays. By his brashness and bravery he had saved many innocents. He was a bold one, her grandfather. And she was of his blood.

Cast thy bread upon the waters: for thou shalt find it after many days.

The verse from Ecclesiastes brought her head upright. She shared with Grandfather a knowing gaze.

Downstairs the tavern entry banged open. Boots tramped the floorboards.

"Search everywhere," a soldier said. "Every room, every bunk."

"Stop," said the innkeeper. "What is this outrage?"

"Have you any lodgers who are not in the king's army?"

"I've boarders upstairs and a tradesman or two. There's also a pair of young women in the attic room with their aged father."

"Fetch them down here."

"Not until I know the reason."

"Fetch them down, you dog, or I'll split your skull."

Already boots hammered the stairs. Doors along the hall below flung open, and furnishings scraped the floorboards. Shouts echoed as guests tumbled from their beds. Grandfather grabbed his cane.

"Well, lasses," he said, reaching through the window and hooking the rope, "if we're Cambridge-bound, now's as good a time as any."

"Through the window?" Sarah said.

" 'Tis the only exit we've got at present."

"But we're three stories up."

32

"And we've a stout elm just beyond the pane. I seem to recall your climbing trees as a girl. Now get you dressed."

Rachel was already stuffing pistols into her pockets. Sarah's face brightened.

"How marvelous," she said.

Four

Cambridge

"I see the shoreline just ahead," Sarah said from the skiff's bow. Hardly had she spoken before the boat scraped the rocky bottom. Grandfather stowed the oars and splashed into the shallows. He dragged the boat onto land and offered a hand to each of the girls.

"There's campfires in the woods ahead," he said. "I expect the rebels have posted sentries along the tree line."

From a pocket he slipped a white linen. After tying it to a stick, he ventured over the slippery stones. Rachel and Sarah clambered after him.

"Ahoy," Grandfather said. "Friends approaching the line."

He waved the white cloth overhead.

"Ahoy," he said again.

"Hold," came a reply. "Who goes there?"

"Patriots from across the bay," Grandfather said. "We've news for Gen. Putnam. Can you take us to him?"

"You wish to see Old Put?"

"Is he nearby?"

"How should I know? Even if he is close about, he's long abed by now. Get you gone and come back on the morrow."

"Our tidings are most urgent," Grandfather said.

The sentry emerged from the woods. A tattered tricorn hat sat crooked on his head, and a farmer's frock hung loose about him. Odors of sweat and filth spewed from his unwashed body. At his waist a long rifle stretched toward Grandfather's belly.

"We've news of the British movements," Grandfather said. The sentry spat.

"No one's moved a yard for two months," he said. "Why start now?"

"Something's afoot," Grandfather said. "We must tell the general straightaway."

"You'll wait until the morrow."

"Tomorrow shall be too late. Why do you think we hazarded a crossing at this hour?"

"That's no concern of mine. Get you gone—before I put a musket ball in your bowels."

"No need for that," Grandfather said. "Come along, lasses. Tomorrow will have to serve."

They retreated to the water's edge.

"What are we to do?" Sarah said, dropping on the boat's rail and plopping her chin in her hands. "Shall we sit here until dawn?"

"I shall try again," Rachel said. "You two remain here."

"What makes you think you will get through?" Sarah said.

"If I am not back by dawn, you may come looking for me."

"But . . ."

"Take this," Grandfather said, extending a loaded pistol to her.

"I've two in my waistband already," she said, patting them.

"Aye, so you do. Very well, then, go with God, lass."

"I hope to."

She wandered the shoreline. A stone's throw from the boat, she turned inland and climbed a large outcrop of rock. Two sentries snored in the crags. All around her crickets chirped and frogs belched. Somewhere an owl hooted. Fireflies winked in the forest, and bats darted overhead. As she sidestepped the sentries, a nearby shrub rustled, startling her. From the thicket waddled a raccoon. She sighed her relief.

Distant campfires brightened the woods, their orange halos barely illuminating scattered bedrolls. Scents of pine perfumed the breezes. She slipped on her mask and wig and gloved her hands, then roamed the black voids separating the camps. Leaves crackled beneath her boots as she trudged the hills and ravines. An occasional stone tripped her, and the spider webs tangling her face made her shudder. Often she paused to listen for footsteps trailing her.

Beyond the forest stretched rolling fields threaded by a road. Tents and dying fires spotted the glades, and stars powdered the heavens. She tramped a furrow of sprouting grain, climbed the stone wall fencing the field, and hiked the highway toward Cambridge. The road's ruts were still soft from spring rains, and she wondered as she walked how to locate Gen. Putnam. Was he berthed in a tent or boarded in a house? The latter seemed more likely, but which house? Doubtless his would be a grand one. Generals always seemed to prefer imposing edifices. Would she creep into each building, beginning with the biggest, and search every bedchamber? That might take all night. And what would a slumbering general look like? Atop his horse and festooned with ribbons he might appear quite marvelous. But abed in the dead of night, with his wig on the bedpost and his teeth on the sideboard, with his bare feet sticking out beyond the sheets and his nose thundering like cannon fire, he might be mistaken for a stable hand.

"Oh, Lord, help me find him," she said. "I wish I *could* hear You speak. Things would go so much easier for both of us. Can You not, just this once, tell me aloud what I wish to know? The task is simple enough for You, surely. Come now, You great God of all creation, whisper to me which house Gen. Putnam's quartered in. Tell me clearly, that I may know You are guiding me."

Stubborn silence surrounded her, and she plodded into Cambridge unenlightened. Hours had passed since she had started her journey, and weariness began to weigh on her. And why shouldn't she be tired? Her adventure had begun with a mad dash across Boston followed by a frantic escape from her lodgings. She recalled the plunge from her bedroom window, spinning down to earth on Grandfather's rope. Sarah had followed, and Grandfather had then lowered his trunk. He let himself down last and slipped the rope from the pulley to mask their means of escape. They were past the hedges and climbing the fence when the soldiers invaded their empty chamber. Grandfather's trunk had proved too heavy to lug to the harbor, so they had hidden it beneath a neighbor's stair. Hopefully it would be there when they returned for it.

"Fool," she said to herself for letting her mind wander. A dozen dwellings had drifted by without her giving one a glance. She turned back, and her eyes fell on a large house surrounded by sentries. Striped flags hung above the entry, and a picket fence alongside corralled a dozen horses. No other building was so adorned.

"I suppose I shan't receive a clearer sign than that," she said. Across the lane and through the alleys she crept to the house's back buildings—a kitchen, a cooper, a smith's forge. At the well she paused to peruse the dwelling. Sentries wandered along the picket fence, but none ventured to the back of the house.

"Those horses," she said. "They may prove useful."

From the soil she scooped several stones, then removed the well's hoisting rope. She pocketed the rocks and carried the cord to the corral. One end she knotted to the gate, and after releasing the latch she threaded the cable across the yard and over the house's back step. The opposite end she wrapped around a rain barrel.

Why were no sentries patrolling the rear entry? Perhaps a guard was posted inside the door. She balanced herself on the rain barrel's brim and wriggled through the open window above it. A long table and chairs told her she had entered the dining room. Embers glowed in the hearth, and on the table's polished surface stood a fruit basket flanked by candelabra. Strewn over the master's chair was a woolen cloak.

She circled the chamber and found it deserted. Her gaze rested on the basket.

"I wonder . . ."

Quickly she plucked out the apples, pears, and grapes and left them littering the table. With the basket and the cloak bundled under an arm, she retreated to the window. Beyond the picket fence a sentry strolled into view. He turned and paced toward the front of the house. She loosened the curtain cords, shoved them into a pocket, and squeezed over the sill to the ground.

Swinging open the corral gate, she slipped into the muddy enclosure. The hinges' squeals brought a guard to the alley. When he reached the fence, she was crouched behind the water trough. A stallion snorted and shook his mane. Other horses complained as the stallion nuzzled them. For several minutes the guard watched them and then returned to the road.

Rachel stuffed the empty basket into the cape's hood and snapped shut the clasp. Cautiously she approached the stallion, stroking his side and slipping the cloak over his back. With a curtain cord she fastened the hooded basket to his neck. The remaining cord she passed beneath his belly and tied both ends to the basket, leaving enough slack to allow the garment to billow over his back.

"You seem a stouthearted steed," she said. "Don't fail me."

Back to the window and into the dining room she crept. Floorboards creaked as she wandered to the hall. A guard slumbered on a bench by the front entrance, his musket leaning against a ticking floor clock. She padded toward him, passing the high-backed chairs lining the walls. As she mounted the stair, the clock chimed. Loud and long it hammered a droll tune and then banged two o'clock. The guard adjusted his hat over his eyes and shifted his perch on the bench. Had he bothered to look up he would have beheld a decayed corpse staring at him from the banister. Instead, he resumed his snoring. She ascended to the upper landing, where a second sentry dozed on the floor. Gathering her skirts, she stepped over him and glided to the end of the hall.

Double doors faced each other from opposite walls. One entry would access a study or parlor, the other a master's bedchamber. She peeked through the right-hand door and perceived a long table piled with documents. The room opposite was crowded by a great bed, its curtains drawn shut. On a bedpost hung a sheathed sword and a tunic with braided shoulder boards.

She eased into the chamber and closed the door. A glance through the open window assured her that the corralled horses were directly below. Drawing back the bed curtain, she gazed down on a sleeping man much younger than she expected. Even in the dark he was clearly tall and robust, with long hair spreading over his pillow. She tugged a pistol from her waistband and prodded him awake.

"What is it?" he said, startled. She pressed the gun's muzzle to his brow.

"Quiet," she said in her toad's voice. "Cry out and you're a dead man."

"Who are you? How did you get past the sentries?"

"I am called Regina Silsby."

"By my soul. Not the Boston ghost."

"I bring tidings of the redcoats' movements. You are in great danger."

"What . . . sort of danger?"

"The British prepare to occupy the heights above Charlestown."

40

"Bunker's Hill?"

"Their field cannons shall be mounted on the bluff by Sunday."

"They've done nothing for months," he said. "How do I know you speak the truth?"

"If you tarry, your positions will be under their guns."

"I cannot do anything without orders from the Committee of Safety."

"Get them. You must not delay."

"But how did you learn of this? What shall I tell them?"

"Sunday," she said, letting the curtain drop. "You have been warned."

"Wait. Please, Regina Silsby, I beg you . . ."

From her pocket she extracted her stones. Reaching through the window, she pelted the horses below. They bellowed and pranced about the pen.

"Don't go," he said. "You mustn't leave."

"Col. Prescott, sir," said a voice beyond the door. "Is something wrong?"

"Sentry," yelled the colonel from his bed. "Come here at once."

Rachel sprang for the entry. Prescott lunged through the bed curtains, arms outstretched. He banged against the window frame and tumbled to the floor. The canopy collapsed on top of him. Rachel darted behind the opening door.

"Col. Prescott, sir."

A guard rushed to the bed. As he fumbled with the curtains, she slipped across the hall to the parlor and pulled shut the door. More guards mounted the stairs.

"Find her," Prescott said.

"Who, sir?"

"Regina Silsby. She was here in the room with me."

"The witch's ghost? But that's impossible, sir. How could she —"

"Turn out the guard at once. She must have gone through the window."

Rachel hurried to a far corner of the chamber. Surely such a large house had a servants' stair. She must find it.

"And send word to Gen. Putnam," Prescott said. "Tell him I'm coming by straightaway. Upon my word, if she's right . . ."

Footsteps pounded the stairs. The rear entry flung open, and a sharp cry followed. That would be a soldier stumbling over her tripwire. If all went well, the corral gate had opened, and . . .

"The horses. They've broken loose."

Thundering hooves confirmed the cry.

"Look there, she's riding off."

A musket boomed.

"Hold your fire," Prescott shouted. "Round up every spare man and get you after her. She mustn't escape."

"But sir, she's mounted."

"Confound you, there's two dozen horses among the New Hampshires. Hurry along."

From a window Rachel watched the mayhem in the street. Officers bellowed and men scrambled in all directions. Prescott bounded through the front entry, shrugging on his topcoat as he marched up the lane. Minutemen surrounded him.

"Time I took my leave," she said. A corner entry accessed a small cupboard with a steep, narrow stair. The ladder descended to a pantry beside the dining room. Scents of cornmeal and cream spawned in her a sharp hunger. While passing the dinner table, she stuffed her pockets with fruit.

The main hall was deserted, its rear door swinging on its hinges.

"Well, why not?" she said, and peeled off her mask and wig. Through the door and down the step she strode, crossing the yard to the lane.

"You there, halt."

She froze. A sentry approached.

"Mercy, lass," he said, "what are you doing out and about?"

"I . . . heard the ruckus," she said. "I thought perhaps . . . I might see . . ."

"Faith, woman, 'tis Regina Silsby up from her grave. Get you home, before she bewitches you."

"Do you mean the Boston sorceress? Gracious, what shall I do if she overtakes me?"

"You should have considered that before you left your dwelling. Now be off."

"Oh, dear. Oh, dear me. Good sir, I don't suppose you would be kind enough to . . ."

". . . see you home? I've my own duties to attend. Get you gone."

"Heavens, she'll put me in my grave before I reach it. Such a fool I've been. Oh my sacred stars, how shall I find my way? Mercy, Lord, please have mercy."

Down a nearby lane she retreated, fretting and wringing her hands as far as the town's fringe. A cart path wandered the fields and forests beyond. She tramped the rutted trail into the hill country, breathing deeply the aromas of barley, hickory, and chestnut. Countless insects sand in leafy canopies.

"Thank You, thank You, thank You," she said, clasping her hands to her chest.

A racket on the roadway forced her into an orchard. Horsemen galloped by. After they had passed, she followed a tunnel of apple trees to the forest. Trails wound through the woods toward the river, and she marched them munching her fruit and pitching sprigs and stems over her shoulder. At the water's edge she traced the shoreline to the skiff.

"Who's there?" Grandfather said.

"It is I, Rachel. I've brought fresh fruits for you."

"How did you fare, lass?"

"The deed's done. Col. Prescott is on his way to see Gen. Putnam even now."

"Good show, child."

"Oh, Rachel, how wonderful," Sarah said, clapping her hands. "How ever did you manage it?"

Five

Bunker's Hill

Maj. Cauldon awakened to cannon fire. He leapt from his bed, tugged on his tunic, and descended the front stair. Soldiers and citizens jammed the streets, peering skyward and shouting excitedly. High overhead the windows, the balconies, and even the rooftops were packed with people staring across the river toward Charlestown.

Cauldon halted a passing soldier.

"You, private, what's going on?" he said.

"Sir, the rebels have taken the heights."

Cauldon's jaw dropped. He dashed into the house, climbed the stairs to his room, and grabbed his spyglass. At the gabled window he threw open the sash and pressed the telescope to his eye.

Scarring the bluff beyond Charlestown were breastworks of freshly turned earth. Hundreds of men shoveled dirt on the mounds, and fences of sharpened stakes surrounded the redoubt. The laborers wore gentlemen's coats, farmer's frocks, and all other manner of motley garb. On a pole in the center of the fort hung a limp flag, and it was no Union Jack. Shells burst on the hillside as warships pummeled the redoubt from the river.

"What's the fuss?" said officers, crowding his back.

"Those wily rebels have taken the heights," he said, snapping shut his glass.

"But how did they . . ."

"Do you expect me to know?"

He pounded down the stairs, and the others tumbled after him. They grabbed hats, coats, swords, and pistols and descended to the street, each man scattering to his own regiment. Cauldon pressed through the mob toward Gen. Gage's headquarters at the Province House.

"About time someone of rank showed up," Gage said. He sat at his desk scribbling orders and shoving parchments toward subordinates, who powdered the ink, folded the papers, and applied wax seals before handing the documents to couriers. Clerks and junior officers proffered sheets needing signatures.

"Tell Admiral Graves I want every available barge at the North Battery," Gage said, while sliding his penned demand to a waiting adjutant. "Where's that list of available artillery?"

Cauldon ignored the bustle and eyed the wall map at Gage's back. Colored pins covered Charlestown peninsula's eastern shore, from the village south to the shoals north.

"I intend to lead a frontal assault against their redoubt," Gage told him.

"Sir," Cauldon said, "may I suggest we first reconnoi-ter—"

"And grant them time to finish their fort? Who's commanding this army, Major, you or I? A show of force will send them running to their homesteads."

"General, sir, such tactics failed us at Concord. We might fare better if we—"

"What was lacking at Concord was sufficient numbers of troops," Gage said. "I shall not repeat the error. Twenty-five hundred men-at-arms will ferry to Charlestown peninsula, supported by field howitzers. By heaven, we shall hurl these bloody rebels into the river."

He handed Cauldon a folded parchment.

"I'm attaching you to the forty-seventh regiment," he said. "You'll be on the left flank with Pitcairn's marines. Get you to the North Battery immediately."

"Aye, sir. Thank you, sir," Cauldon said, saluting. He turned on his heel and marched from the house. Already his uniform was damp with sweat. Was it the summer heat or the anticipation of battle and the chance to patch his wounded pride? Through the crowds he waded to his lodgings. There he buckled on his sword, shoved a pair of pistols into his belt, and pocketed a handful of cartridges. After gulping a mouthful of cider, he returned to the street and hurried toward the waterfront.

The North Battery's wharves were a confusion of bellowing officers, rapping drums, droning bagpipes, and trilling fifes. Grenadiers, light infantry, fusiliers, marines, and artillerymen all tangled in a teeming, scarlet mass. Flags of every hue and pattern marked the units' gathering points. With maddening slowness the ranks took shape as each man found his place and stood stiffly in line, his pack strapped to his back and his musket pressed to his side. Sergeants inspected rucksacks, checked firearms, sorted cartridges, and straightened uniforms. Along the quays rumbled horse teams towing field cannons. Gun crews wrestled powder kegs and shot to the water's edge. Hoists were rigged and tackle greased. Waiting barges banged against the docks.

Overhead the Copp's Hill battery thundered. Shells screamed across the harbor and burst on the hillside below the fort. Warships anchored in the river also belched smoke and flame.

"Too high, that ridge," said an officer at Cauldon's elbow. "The ships can't elevate their guns enough."

"And the shore batteries are too distant," Cauldon said. "All this bombast is wasted."

" 'Twill be up to us, then, eh, Major? Not to worry, we'll ferret them out quick enough."

"Curse this sultry weather," soldiers said. " 'Tis hotter than a witch's oven."

"Push on," others said. "What's the delay?"

"Hold your tongues," Cauldon said. "You'll have at them soon enough."

Longboats and cutters clogged the wharves. The troops, burdened by their hundred-pound packs, struggled down rope nets strung along the seawall and tumbled into the vessels.

"Move along," Cauldon bellowed. "You there, mind your step, or you'll have everyone in the water with you. Hold up, private. Fall out and strap on that mess kit better. You, where's your bayonet? And why is this canteen empty? Who

48

gave you permission to drink your whole ration? Sergeant, take this man's name."

Rank after rank of scarlet troops descended the nets and crammed into the boats. With much swearing and snarling, Cauldon's soldiers packed themselves into a stout barge, their muskets bristling above them like porcupine quills. When the last man had squeezed between the rails, Cauldon struggled into the stern sheets and ordered the coxswain to shove off.

"Release mooring cables," said the helmsman. "Starboard sweeps, fend off."

The barge lumbered from the pier. Barefooted seamen heaved at the oars, and the vessel lurched toward open water.

Screeching gulls circled the barge as it pitched and rolled beneath a blistering sun. Other boats churned from the jetties and wallowed on the harbor waves. Church steeples tolled quarter-past noon, then half-past, and three-quarters past. One o'clock chimed, and still the flotilla sloshed about the harbor. Sweat streaked sunburned faces and stung bleached eyes. For the hundredth time Cauldon tugged his timepiece from his waistcoat, fuming at the delay.

Half-past one o'clock tolled, and at last the fleet ventured across the harbor. Longboats packed with marines joined Cauldon's barge as it plied past booming warships. Instinctively the troops ducked as cannonballs screamed over their heads and sucked drafts of hot wind after them. Sulfur haze lingered on the water, poisoning the air with burnt brimstone. The boats emerged from the yellow fog and scraped ashore at a rocky beach just east of the town.

"Disembark," Cauldon said. "Form up at the road there. Sergeant, take a detachment into Charlestown and scout it. Report any activity to me."

"Aye, sir."

Relieved to be on solid ground again, Cauldon marched about inspecting his ranks. Illness plagued most of the troops, and the weight of their packs added to their misery. Gladly he would have ordered the excess equipment dropped until after the battle. Without their loads the men would quickly regain their vigor and overwhelm the rebel positions. But Gage was issuing no such command. His troops assembled on the beach in full kits.

"Blind fool," Cauldon said under his breath. Swarms of insects assailed the men. Buzzards mocked them, and hot sun broiled them from a cloudless sky.

"Major, sir," said a scout, "Charlestown is deserted."

"The entire city?" Cauldon said.

"Fled the naval bombardment, sir, that's my wager. There's a lot of activity behind the town on Charlestown Neck."

"Coming or going?"

"Both, sir."

Drums sounded from Gage's position.

"The grenadiers are moving forward," Cauldon said. "Sergeant, you'd better return your men to their ranks. Forty-seventh, prepare to advance."

Through his spyglass Cauldon watched Gage's regiments cross the base of the hill. The spectacle was daunting, even dreadful, as rank upon rank of scarlet troops trampled the fields, bayonets glinting in the sun. Cauldon ordered his own soldiers forward, aligning the regiment with Gage's left flank. The completed lines seemed a mile long.

Abruptly the drumming ceased, and the troops halted. Stiffly, silently, they ringed the hill, waist deep in golden grass. Around them crickets chirped and bees hummed.

Cawing crows hopped the stone walls threading the rise. A pair of hawks circled overhead, and seagulls settled on the empty barges lining the shore. Sailors trundled howitzers into position along the seaside road. Beside each cannon the gun crews heaped powder charges and shells, and spread tarpaulins over them.

"Where's the need for field guns, Major?" said a man at Cauldon's elbow. "We'll put those mongrels in their places soon enough."

"Old Gage likes his battles prim and proper," said another.

"He's not one to take chances."

"Silence in the ranks," Cauldon said.

"Major, sir, we've men aplenty for that pup's den yonder. Let's go at them and be done with it."

"Hold your tongue," Cauldon said. "Do you think you're the only man wanting a taste of rebel blood? Mind your place and wait your turn."

"They'll be nothing left of them when the cannoning's done."

"We'll advance when we're ordered."

Howitzers roared. Their smoke drifted through the soldiers' ranks. As the haze cleared, the drums resumed their thumping.

"Forty-seventh, advance," Cauldon said. His troops waded into the grass. At thirty paces the drums signaled a second halt. Once more the field guns boomed.

"Companies, present arms."

Cauldon repeated the order. His regiment raised their muskets toward the top of the ridge. The motion was repeated along the line until a wall of weaponry hemmed the hill.

"Fire."

Thunder shook the bluff, and smoke swallowed the crimson lines. The drums resumed.

"Forty-seventh, advance," Cauldon said. His ranks toiled through the grass and climbed over a stone wall. At thirty paces Gage's drummers signaled another halt.

"What in heaven's name is he thinking?" Cauldon said as another artillery barrage pounded the fort. Any fool could see the cannon fire was useless, and the musketry even less so.

Shots sounded at his regiment's rear. A soldier fell. Cauldon wheeled about. Windows among the Charlestown dwellings puffed smoke.

"Third Company, halt," he said. "Captain, take the rest of the regiment forward. I shall remain here with the detachment."

"Aye, sir."

"Third Company, about face."

The soldiers turned toward the houses. Cauldon ordered muskets primed and loaded.

"Present," he said. "Mark the windows and fire."

Bullets spattered the buildings.

"Reload," Cauldon said. "Handle your cartridges and prime."

Warships in the harbor swung slowly on their anchor cables, easing their broadsides toward the town. Cannon muzzles appeared in open gun ports. The hulls vanished in clouds of smoke. Clapboard walls splintered, windows shattered, chimneys crumbled. Ragged scars holed the structures, seeping smoke. Again the ships battered the buildings. Several structures erupted in flames.

"They've set the city afire," said a man in Cauldon's ranks.

"Three cheers for the king's navy."

The men shouted hurrahs. Black smoke soon poured from the snipers' windows.

"Company, about face," Cauldon said. "Quick march. We'll rejoin the regiment."

His soldiers huffed up the hill toward their comrades. Twenty paces from the breastworks another halt was ordered. A final volley pummeled the fort. Through the dissipating smoke came the long-expected order: "Bayonets at the ready. Prepare to assault the redoubt."

Cauldon marveled at the silence of the rebel positions. Their flag hung limp on its pole, as listless as the mongrels huddling behind the earthen mounds. What was their plan? Had they one at all? Or had the bombardment done its murderous work?

"Companies, charge the redoubt."

Drums beat the final assault.

"Advance!" Cauldon yelled. "Now we'll see these peasant farmers flee."

With a great shout the crimson lines hurtled forward. The troops descended a ditch surrounding the fort and climbed the breastworks. Sharp stakes and a high fence blunted their assault. Rear ranks tangled with those forward. A single command sounded from the rebel position.

The redoubt exploded. Smoke swallowed the earthen mounds, and a howl swept the hillside. Great gaps holed the British lines.

"Keep your formations," Cauldon shouted. "Captains, rally your men."

Entire regiments disintegrated. Drummers fell, colors collapsed. Shrieking men fled down the slope, stampeding over
the low walls and tumbling through the tall grass. Cauldon
grabbed the regimental flag and held it aloft.

"Rally!" he yelled, waving the banner over his head.
Shots peppered the fabric. He watched in amazement as the
entire army, over two thousand strong, melted before him.
Crimson-coated bodies littered the hillside. Gage's command
position was abandoned by all but the dead men sprawled at
their posts.

Frantically Cauldon pursued his comrades down the hill,
cursing as he leapt walls and fences. At the seaside road he
thrust the flag into a soldier's hands and snagged a fleeing
drummer.

"Sound formation," he said. The lad bawled huge tears.
Cauldon pressed a pistol to the boy's brow.

"Sound formation," he said, "or I shall blow out your
brains."

The threat paralyzed the drummer into compliance, and
he beat the signal to reform. Everywhere troops squealed like
babies. Many cast aside their weapons and packs and flung
themselves into the barges.

"Rally!" Cauldon shouted. "Reform your ranks."

He marched along the beach, clubbing men with his pistol.

"Cowards," he said. "You call yourselves king's men? Get
back in rank."

Sergeants bludgeoned soldiers into formation. Farther
up the beach Gage's officers brutally reorganized their own
ranks. Black smoke spewing from the Charlestown blaze
rolled along the shore.

"You men there, form up," Cauldon said. "Are you planning to swim back to Boston? Form your ranks, you louts."

Soldiers were beaten from the boats and forced into line. Those who had thrown away their muskets stood without them.

"You can find one as we advance," Cauldon said, "and if some rebel crushes your skull before you can arm yourself, 'twill be your own fault."

At last the army was reassembled. Drummers beat the signal to advance, and the troops climbed the hill, wading through heaps of fallen bodies. As before, the lines halted every thirty paces. Artillery barrages preceded volleys of musketry. A second bayonet charge collapsed at the breastworks, and once more the rebels' fury hurled the scarlet columns down the hill.

Rachel stood on the upper balcony of the Hawkins' boarding house clutching a kerchief to her breast. Beside her Sarah leaned on the rail bouncing excitedly. Grandfather was perched on a stool behind two elderly ladies, his spyglass trained northward. All about them spectators jammed rooftops and windows. Even church belfries sprouted onlookers, and distant Beacon Hill was cluttered with carriages and crowds.

Across the river Charlestown poured black smoke into the sky. Flaming church spires collapsed one by one into the inferno. Beyond the blaze stretched the carnage of Bunker's Hill. Twice the redcoats had assaulted the redoubt, and twice they had been repulsed. Crimson carcasses littered the ridge, and still the stubborn ranks amassed for a third assault. The British army seemed half its original size.

"My heavens," said one of the women at Rachel's back, "to think such brave soldiers should fall by the hands of those despicable wretches."

"There's not a man in that mob who can call himself a gentleman," said her companion. "How mortifying that they speak the same language as we and can trace themselves from English stock."

"A most ungrateful and degenerate lot they are."

"The redcoats are at it again," Grandfather said. All eyes turned toward the bluff. Up the hill the army marched, cannons thundering, muskets clattering. For some reason the redoubt did not reply, and the scarlet ranks poured over the breastworks.

"The rebels are getting the worst of it," Grandfather said while squinting through his spyglass. "They're falling back. I've never seen a sharper action."

"Miserable demons, these country bandits," said the first woman. " 'Tis a pity more of them haven't been killed."

"The rebels are off the hill," Grandfather said. "They're retreating to Charlestown Neck."

"Tell me, sir, do the soldiers pursue them? Such pirates cannot be allowed to escape."

"Appears to me the redcoats have had enough of fighting," Grandfather said. "They're staying atop the hill, firing down on the rebels from the redoubt."

"Gracious," said the woman. "All will be for naught if the devils get away. Really, something must be done to rid us of these pests. They should be slaughtered, every one of them."

Rachel turned from the rail and retreated into the house. Distant musketry rattled her ears as she descended the stair.

In the solitude of her chamber, she collapsed on her bed and wept.

Six

In Conference

"Gen. Gage, sir, our scouts confirm the presence of rebel strongholds on all the hills west of Charlestown Neck."

Gage's frown deepened. He sat at the head of a long table surrounded by uniformed officers. Sunlight streamed through the open windows.

"So," he said, "Bunker's Hill has gained us nothing."

"Sir, I beg to differ," said a rotund colonel with flabby jowls. "We took the hill. You have a victory."

"A victory that cost half my force. And still we cannot get out of Boston."

"But neither can the rebels get in, sir."

"A stalemate, Colonel—how very comforting."

"The harbor is safe at any rate. We should be glad of that."

"Are you blind, sir? On Bunker's Hill we suffered a thousand casualties, and not one thing has changed. Too many more victories of that kind, and we shall lose this war."

"Our troops conducted themselves valiantly on difficult ground, sir," the colonel said. "I thought the entire operation exceedingly soldier-like, nearly perfect. And the forces opposing us were easily twice our size. I myself saw fresh reinforcements marching across Charlestown Neck by thousands and—"

"Colonel, we have since learned that the rebels were half our number—and probably less. It appears, gentlemen, that two thousand of his majesty's finest troops were almost destroyed by seven hundred farmers. Had the enemy not run out of gunpowder, they'd be bombarding us even now. And need I remind you that Fort Ticonderoga has already fallen to the rebels? This very moment sixty artillery pieces may be on their way to Boston."

"But sir, without powder—"

"Confound it, man," Gage said, "these crafty rebels shall probably contrive a way to steal it from us."

He scowled as the implication of his words settled on his staff. Defeat—that most improbable of outcomes—had almost overtaken them. But for a few pounds of gunpowder, the rebels would have repulsed the third assault on Bunker's Hill, and the surviving regiments would not have mustered enough will or means to make a fourth. Rebel artillery would now be raining shot and shell on the harbor, scattering the warships, forcing the soldiers to their transports for evacuation and disgrace—all for want of a few pounds of powder.

"Major Cauldon," Gage said. "You seem eager to speak."

"Begging your pardon, sir. I meant no offense."

"Share your thoughts with us."

"I hardly think the opinions of a lowly major are worth mentioning in this company, sir."

"I insist, Major. Speak your mind."

"Very well, sir," Cauldon said, swallowing. "If I may be so bold, I see no reason for us to remain in Boston at all."

"Insolent," said the colonel. "Are you suggesting we evacuate? Would you have us run like beaten dogs after a victory so dearly bought? What nonsense are you blathering?"

"With all respect, Colonel," Cauldon said, "the port is useless to us if we cannot make offensive thrusts into the country. We should employ the position or abandon it."

"Would you have us admit by such action," said the colonel, "that Great Britain can be bested by a pack of peasants?"

"I humbly suggest, sir, that our own folly occasioned this terrible loss."

"Impertinent, sir. How dare you make such a wild accusation before your commanding officers."

"Gen. Gage asked me to speak my mind," Cauldon said. "I'm sure the general prefers candor to flattery."

"Go on," Gage said.

"Had we first scouted the terrain," Cauldon said, "we would have seen how easily our troops might have landed in the rebels' rear and trapped them on the peninsula. The heights upon Charlestown Neck are higher than the hill occupied by the rebels, and we could have rained shot on them without losing a single soldier. By such a move we would have forced them to surrender or be blown to pieces. Instead we chose a frontal assault, exposing our troops to their fire, and leaving the enemy rear open for their escape across the

Neck. The action cost us a thousand of our best men and has given the rebels great reason to exult over us."

"Indeed," said another major, "the rebels are now spirited by more rage and enthusiasm than any people ever possessed."

"Never did they show such vigor against the French," said the colonel. "Yet against us, their own countrymen, they conjure from within themselves demons more fierce than hell's worst. And they don't fight like gentlemen. Scoundrels, that's what they are, shooting officers from behind walls as they do."

"The rebels merely employ whatever is to their advantage," Cauldon said, "just as we should."

"We'd have done better," said a captain, "to follow them across the isthmus, instead of remaining on the hill. The rebels were out of powder. We could have—"

" 'Tis pointless," Cauldon said, "to carp now on what should have been done. We must either proceed in earnest from here or give the business up. I, for one, do not wish to give up any business once I've begun it. 'Tis true the rebels outnumber us, but they are disorganized. We may use that to our advantage."

"And what do you propose, Major?" Gage said. "A small army such as ours cannot prevail. We must have large bodies of men, making diversions on different sides and dividing their forces."

"Sir, we have the rivers and coastal waters available to us. We could ferry light infantry to their flanks and assault them from their sides and rear."

"Such a course would merely divide our meager forces," Gage said, "and provide the enemy an opportunity to destroy us piecemeal. No, sir, to reduce this people we shall need a great force."

"Sir," Cauldon said, "mustering such armies may take a year or more. We must act now with whatever means is available to us. Either we seize the momentum, or yield it to the rebels."

"Poppycock," said the fat colonel. "The rebels dare not enter Boston, and there's been no trouble elsewhere. What more is wanted?"

"If a man is defending his house," Cauldon said, "should he wait for the robber to invade his property, or should he hunt the robber at his lair and strike him first?"

Gage leaned his head in his hands.

"Would it were so simple," he said. "Troops must be supplied, lines of communication guarded, signals determined. Your parable is effective for one man, Major, but for moving of large masses of troops . . ."

"It can be done, sir," Cauldon said. "It must be done. Our only alternative is to wait for the rebels to attack. You said yourself that Ticonderoga's guns are coming against us. Either we evacuate Boston now, or we wait until the guns arrive and force us out. I say we seize the initiative now. Let us use the waterways to confound the rebels with swift, sudden moves. Who knows? We may even recapture the stolen cannons."

Several majors nodded their agreement, but the fat colonel scoffed. Gage pressed his fingers to his lips.

"You seem full of youthful energies, Maj. Cauldon," he said. "Such vigor requires a task suitable to its . . . strengths. Are you up to such a challenge?"

"Your servant, sir."

"We've a spy among us."

"Sir?"

"I don't mean here, at this table. Have you ever heard of Regina Silsby?"

Eyebrows jumped.

"A local legend, isn't she?" Cauldon said. "Demon ghost of some sort."

"She's come back to haunt us."

"I don't understand, sir."

"Our grenadiers observed her in the town," Gage said, "terrorizing a tallow merchant or some such."

"How does that concern us?" Cauldon said.

"I've reason to believe she learned our plans for Bunker's Hill and alerted the rebels."

"Sir, why would a ghost . . ."

"She's not a ghost, Major; she's a rebel spy. Only last year she threw our entire garrison into confusion. I think it most curious that on the very day I inform my officers of our plans for Bunker's Hill, she not only shows her face but enables the rebels to employ against us the very plan we intended to carry out against them. Regina Silsby is the reason we suffered so heavily on Bunker's Hill, gentlemen. She is the reason we are trapped in Boston now. I want her found and hanged, do you hear? The sooner the better."

"Sir," Cauldon said, "this task seems more appropriate for a junior officer. May I suggest—"

"You wanted something to do, Major, and you shall have it. Somehow that ghost knows everything we do. There's not a plan we can devise that is safe while she's about. Were we to venture into the waterways as you propose, we would find ourselves sailing into ambush after ambush. Until she's caught, all our efforts are jeopardized. I want her found, Maj. Cauldon. Use any means at your disposal, but bring me Regina Silsby's head. Understood?"

"Perfectly, sir. How shall I know her?"

"She's the ugliest hag this side of Hades."

Seven

Spies

"I know a simple way out of Boston," Sarah said. She was perched on a bench by the town gate, cradling a ball of yarn in her lap. Rachel sat knitting beside her, her face shielded beneath a straw summer bonnet. Its wide brim was pressed to her cheeks by ribbons laced beneath her chin. Sarah, with only a lace cap crowning her golden hair, freely observed everything.

For two weeks the girls had posted themselves about Boston, hoping to catch a glimpse of Rachel's brother, trying to remain unobserved by everyone else. The task was difficult with one so vivacious as Sarah. Her smile dazzled all the soldiers, who greeted her with blushes and bows. Gifts of food and drink came at her from every direction, and she received them all with thanks and flatteries. During her moments alone, which were few, she sang songs to herself, especially those circulating among the Boston patriots.

How brave ye went out with your muskets all bright,
And thought to be-frighten the folks with the sight.
But when you got there how they powdered your pums,
And all the way home how they peppered your bums.
And do you not think it a comical crack,
To be proud in the face and be shot in the back?

Sarah's was the only sunny countenance in Boston. All others were sullen, despondent, grim. Soldiers drilled daily on vacant lots formerly occupied by manors. Churches were stripped of their pews and converted to hospitals and horse stables. Uniformed ruffians invaded houses and carried off furniture, beds, linens, draperies—anything of value. Abandoned dwellings were stripped apart for firewood. Animal carcasses that would not have been touched in the street sold at market for eight pence per pound. Salt provisions, when they could be found, left such a foul taste and so burning a thirst that even the most desperate loathed to eat them. Everyone ate them. Gallows and gibbets were strung with deserters in every public square, and daily funeral processions meandered to all the burial grounds. From sunup to sundown the girls observed every activity, watched every person, studied every face. None resembled Rachel's brother.

"There are lots of people coming and going through that gate without a pass," Sarah said. "All of them are running some errand for the army. One fellow's bartering for provisions; another's getting fuel. I heard this last man say he's going fishing off the Cambridge shore, and he promised to sell his catch to the British commissary. That sentry's letting them all by. We shall make a similar excuse and slip right through."

"Perhaps we should try straightaway," Rachel said, "before the guard's changed."

"And abandon your brother Robert?"

"I'm beginning to doubt he is in Boston at all."

"Ah, Miss Sarah, there you are," said a voice. "I found you at last."

Across the square strolled a youthful officer trailed by several comrades. Instinctively Sarah flashed a sunny smile. Rachel buried her face in her knitting.

"I've been searching all about town for you, Miss Sarah," the officer said. "You remember me, don't you? We spoke in Orange Street three days ago."

"Gracious," Sarah said, "so many handsome men I've met since coming to Boston. Let me see, you are . . . you are . . ."

"John Styles, captain to his majesty's fifth regiment."

"Aye, of course. You like to call yourself Jack."

"No," he said, "you must mean someone else."

His companions smirked and nudged one another.

"Certainly not, Captain," she said, "I am teasing you, of course. No gentleman with manners so fine as yours would call himself Jack. And you've brought friends along with you."

"The same fellows I had with me last time."

"Indeed?" she said. "But you were so noble yourself that I hardly noticed them."

"Miss Sarah, may I present Captain Richards, also of the fifth, and Lieutenants Mallory and Kite."

The men swept off their hats and bowed low.

"Charmed," she said. "Please allow me to introduce to you my cousin, Rachel."

"Heavens, she's a shy one," Styles said, stooping to peek under her bonnet. "Hello, in there."

"Hello," Rachel said, leaning lower into her work.

"Pay her no mind," Sarah said. "She's got to finish this shawl by next week for our aunt's birthday, so she's quite busy with it. Tell us, Capt. Styles, how goes the siege?"

"Wednesday we were off on a skirmish up the Mystic River," he said. "Lots of shooting but nothing decisive. The rebels fight like timid hounds. They're all bark and bluster, but at the first sign of real trouble they flee into the woods."

"Sniveling cowards," Sarah said.

"Last night they floated two batteries off the Cambridge shore and fired into the camp on the common. Did you hear the cannoning, Miss Sarah?"

"Aye, we wondered what the noise was about. Was anyone hurt?"

"No," Styles said, "but they did pepper a tent or two. The lads are hoping it won't rain."

He laughed at his joke, and she joined him.

"Miss Sarah," he said, "I've wonderful news. A supply ship's just come in from the Gardner's Islands. There's two thousand live sheep aboard, plus oxen, butter, eggs and all manner of fine foods, even sherry and port wines. We're to have a party tonight among the officers at the Prospect House on Beacon Street, with a comedy afterwards."

"A comedy?"

"Nothing professional, you understand, just a little farce put together by some of the fellows."

"How can you have time for comedies, with all those rebels festering at the gates?"

"Gage hasn't got us doing much else at present. We must pass the time somehow. What say you, Miss Sarah? Won't you join us? 'Twill be a wonderful lark."

"Really, sir, on such short notice—"

"We'd love to go," Rachel said, looking Styles full in the face. Her outburst startled everyone.

"Good heavens," Styles said, "the girl's got a tongue, after all. Look you, lads, she's quite pretty, too. May I ask, Miss . . ."

"Jennifer."

". . . Miss Jennifer . . . I beg your pardon, but didn't Miss Sarah say before that your name was . . ."

"Jennifer," Rachel said. "That is what I prefer to be called."

"Well, Miss Jennifer, where may we call upon you and your charming cousin?"

"We are sisters, Captain."

"But I thought she said . . ."

"Did I?" Sarah said. "Dear me, I was just . . . I mean, we were just visiting our cousins yesterday, were we not, sister? The word must have slipped from my mouth. Rachel is my sister . . . I mean, Jennifer is my sister. Goodness, your invitation has so excited me that I can hardly talk."

"I'm glad that I can produce so profound a reaction," Styles said. "Where may we call upon you both?"

The girls exchanged a glance.

"Dock Square," Rachel said, "near Faneuil Hall."

The captain arched an eyebrow.

"Our dwelling is such a shambles," she said. "We couldn't bear to have you see it."

"You're not hiding a husband from us, are you, Miss Jennifer?"

"Gracious," she said, "what makes you think me so wicked?"

"Terribly sorry. I simply cannot believe that two such pretty girls haven't married."

"We have not yet encountered the proper gentlemen," Sarah said. "Perhaps you know a suitable pair, Captain."

"Ah, Miss Sarah," he said, beaming. "May we call for you at half-past six?"

"We shall await you at the square," she said.

"And we shall look forward to it," Styles said. "A very good day to you, Miss Sarah, Miss Jennifer."

"And to you, Captain," Sarah said. "Fare you well."

The soldiers tipped their hats and strolled away, congratulating themselves.

"Rachel," Sarah said, "what on earth are you about?"

"We may learn something from them. Any news could be useful."

"You're just looking for a decent meal."

"Don't pretend that you wouldn't like one. We can stuff our skirts full of things for Grandfather as well."

"Mercenary, that's what you are."

"What about you, toying with that poor man's affections? 'I remember you. You like to call yourself Jack.' Really, Sarah."

" 'Twas a good guess. And what of your falsehoods, Miss Jennifer?"

"Grandfather uses a disguised name. We should too. And remember we're supposed to be sisters, not cousins. 'Tis part of our ruse."

"I keep forgetting."

"You'll get us into trouble if you're not careful. The last thing we want is to draw attention to ourselves."

"Why, then, are we attending a ball?"

"Where else will we find a host of British officers eager to boast about their doings? We shall keep our eyes and ears open to everything and treat our bellies to a good stuffing besides."

"But we haven't a decent dress between us," Sarah said.

"We must find something."

Eight

❧

The Comedy

"Spies?" Grandfather said, smacking his brow. He dropped onto his stool by the window.

"We may learn something useful," Rachel said.

"Where did you get those dresses?"

"I bartered a day's housekeeping to the Endicotts next door," she said. "What do you think?"

"You'll be the toast of the party," he said, "and heaven help us all. When did you find time to do your hair so prettily?"

"This afternoon while you were out and about. Sarah's quite good at it."

"Saints alive."

He grabbed his pipe and stuffed tobacco into the bowl. The girls, lacking time for modesty, stripped to their camisoles and wriggled into hoops and gowns. Sarah's dress was lime green brocade with lace adorning its sloping neckline and sleeves. Rachel wrapped herself in lavender satin. All the while Grandfather fixed his gaze beyond the window, his lips pursed, his pipe belching smoke.

"There, 'tis done," Rachel said. "How do we look?"

"Magnificent," he said. "Were I thirty years younger, I'd be chasing after you myself. Now get you gone before I take my cane to your wanton hides. Insolent, that's what you are."

"Grandfather, you old rogue," Rachel said. "What of all your reckless adventures? Were you a girl, you'd be doing just as we are."

" 'Tis a hornet's nest you're wandering into."

"We shall be careful."

"Even so, take these with you."

He dug into his sea chest and handed each girl a pistol.

"Tuck them into your hoop pockets," he said. "Both are loaded and set to half-cock. If any of them redcoats gets brazen with you, put a musket ball into his skull."

"We shan't be harmed," Rachel said, accepting the pistol and kissing his cheek.

"You fret too much," Sarah said. She pressed her lips to his brow and added, "Thank you for doing so."

"I don't like this," he said, "not a wee bit."

" 'Twill be fun," Sarah said, lifting her skirts and burying the pistol beneath her hoops. After rearranging her gown, she followed Rachel to the stair.

"My goodness," said a voice from across the corridor. "Has the sun risen twice today?"

Old Col. Dowd stood in the doorway opposite, his girth as wide as the entry, his shoes off, his waistcoat unbuttoned, his cravat untied, his wig askew. In one hand sloshed a half-empty tankard of wine; in the other drooped a gnawed chunk of mutton.

"You ladies look fit for a king's ball," he said. "What's the occasion?"

"Good evening, Colonel," Sarah said with a curtsey. "We're invited to dine with officers from the fifth regiment."

"Not that fawning Lord Percy?"

"No one so grand as he," she said. "Only captains and lieutenants."

"What's to be gained by dining with juniors," he said, "when you've a senior officer available in your own lodgings? Come to the parlor with me, and we'll have a jaw over some supper."

"I'm sure you've better ways to pass your evening than with two silly girls," she said.

"I cannot think of anything I'd rather do."

"You're too kind, sir. Any other evening we would be glad to accept your generous offer."

"You'll be missing a merry time at games and singing," he said. "Bless my soul, to have the both of you under the same roof makes me giddy as a youngster."

"Colonel, I'll not decline you," Grandfather said, swatting the fat man's back. "Let's go down together, you and I, and see what our landlord's got in the larder. And let me warn you, sir, that only today I have learned a brand-new ditty, a real snapper."

"Indeed," the colonel said with dampened enthusiasm. Grandfather hooked the colonel's arm and urged him down the stairs.

"You're sure you won't join us," the colonel said as the girls escaped through the front entry.

"Good bye," Sarah said, waving. "You needn't wait up for us."

She descended the steps with Rachel and scooted around the corner. Hardly had they sat on a tavern bench when a coach-and-four clattered into the square.

"Gracious," Sarah said. "Such dignified conveyance. Wherever did you gentlemen find it?"

" 'Tis the former governor's," Styles said as he popped open the door. "He was in such haste to retreat to London that he left it behind."

Sarah waved to Mallory and Kite, who stood on the footman's bench between the rear wheels. They returned her greeting, clearly disappointed to be riding behind rather than inside. An enlisted man was perched on the driver's box.

"I feel myself a duchess," Sarah said, accepting the hand Styles offered her.

"And so shall you be tonight," he said. "You remember Capt. Richards, don't you?"

"Indeed."

She sat opposite Richards, gaped at his tunic, and said, "So many ribbons and medals. What do they all mean?"

"Very little, really," he said. "Some of them I can't even recall. Let me see, this one's for . . ."

His voice trailed off as Rachel slipped into the carriage. She sat beside Sarah, arranged her skirts, and teased the dark tresses gathered at her neck.

"Gracious, Miss Jennifer," he said. "You're magnificent."

"Thank you, Captain," she said, unaccustomed to any attention when Sarah was nearby. "Where did you say you were taking us? The Prospect House?"

"Just so," Styles said, leaping into the coach and banging shut the door. He thumped the tip of his scabbard on the carriage roof and said, "Driver, to the Prospect House, and be quick about it."

The carriage jolted forward.

"Miss Jennifer," Richards said, "how goes your shawl? Will it be finished in time for your aunt's birthday?"

"I surely hope so," she said. "Did you pass your afternoon well?"

"We took three townsmen from the Christ Church steeple," Styles said. "They were signaling our condition to the enemy on the far shores and confessed to doing so for a fortnight."

"What will become of them?"

"A hanging, most likely. I fished from the river one fellow who was swimming over to the rebels. He'll be executed in a day or two."

"Our troops are badly vexed," Richards said, "but I'm sure that's no surprise, even to you ladies. We live on salt pork and fish mostly, all of it hard as wood. Our only beverages are rum and spruce liquor, and these throw the men into such fits of flux that they're left looking like skeletons. We bury our dead thirty at a time in trenches, with nary a church bell to toll their passing."

"Where will it all end?" Rachel said.

"We've got to find a way to break this blockade," he said, "or lose every man in our army to scurvy and smallpox.

Heaven knows we've done sufficient penance for all the sins of our lives."

"Richards, you're as gloomy as a graveyard," Styles said. "A supply ship's come in, the first of many, we expect, and tonight we shall make merry by it."

The carriage rolled to a stop at a Beacon Hill mansion.

"Footman," Styles said. "See to the door for us, handsomely now. What say you, ladies? We really should make a proper entrance, don't you think?"

"Is it proper to treat your fellow officers as servants?" Rachel said.

"They're not fellow officers," Styles said. "They're lieutenants, one grade below us."

"Were you not a lieutenant once?"

"By my faith, so I was. What are you saying, Miss Jennifer?"

"Do unto others as you would have them do unto you, Capt. Styles."

"Listen to her, will you, Richards? We've a candidate for sainthood in our midst."

"Indeed," Richards said. Mallory pulled open the carriage door, and Styles assisted Sarah to the pavement.

"Thank you, my man," Styles said to Mallory. "You'll await us at the carriage, of course."

The lieutenant's face fell.

"I thought they were joining us," Rachel said to Richards.

"So did I. Perhaps Styles wishes not to be robbed of Miss Sarah's attentions."

"Selfish brute."

"Richards, hurry on," Styles said over his shoulder. "You're bringing up the rear too slowly."

"We'll be along," Richards said. "Miss Jennifer, you've struck my sensibilities. You're right; it isn't proper that we enjoy a gay evening while the men suffer so. Tomorrow, I shall begin attending better to the welfare of my men. No . . . on second thought, I shall begin tonight."

He turned to the carriage.

"Mallory, Kite," he said. "You'll be joining us, won't you?"

"Aye, sir, thank you, sir," they said, scampering forward. "Thank you very much indeed."

"First, you must fetch something back to our coachman there."

"Aye, sir, that's very good of you, sir. He'll be most grateful."

"Gracious," Rachel said, "to find one considerate man is rare enough. But to enjoy the company of three is almost more than I can bear."

"Your servant, miss," they said, bowing and doffing their hats. She took a lieutenant on each arm and strolled between them to the entry.

"I admire men who take pity on their fellows," she said. "It tells me they shall make good husbands."

"Thank you very much, miss."

The house's rooms were sumptuous. Chandeliers of polished brass brightened the chambers, and delicately patterned fabric covered the walls from chair back to ceiling. A stringed quartet played softly in a parlor adjoining the dining room, where long tables overflowed with plates of lamb, fish, fruits, potatoes, and buttered beans. Bowls of spiced punch crowded the sideboards, and liveried stewards proffered trays of drink and delicacies. The men crowding the rooms were all uniformed in red, their shoulders decorated with braided cords, their breasts sprouting medallions, their sashes dangling swords. Without exception the ladies were young and alluring.

"Styles, Richards, what have you brought among us?" said a major, spilling cider from his tankard.

"Maj. Marsten," Styles said, "I have the greatest pleasure of presenting to you Miss Sarah and her sister Miss Jennifer."

"Charmed," Marsten said. "We've emptied the drawing room of its furniture for dancing. I do hope you'll honor me with a turn."

"I shall very much look forward to it, Major," Sarah said with a curtsey. "Already I can see you'll make a most delightful partner."

Rachel marveled at Sarah's social prowess. Within minutes she had every officer in the house feeding from her palm like so many birds. They followed her in flocks from room to room, offering meats and wines, blushing at her steady flow of compliments, and begging repeatedly for dances or strolls in the garden. For the first time, Rachel realized that Sarah won her adoration by looking each man in the eye and convincing him that she had noticed no one else.

"Richards, will you introduce me to this fair flower on your arm?"

"Maj. Cauldon," Richards said, startled. "Please forgive my bad manners, sir. I'm most pleased to present Miss Jennifer . . . Miss Jennifer . . ."

"Gooding," Rachel said, extending her hand. "How do you do, Major?"

"Much better now, thank you," he said, kissing her fingers. "Do you reside here in Boston, Miss Jennifer, or have you come in from the surrounding country?"

His voice sounded familiar.

"My sister and I have only just arrived," she said. "Tell me, Major, have we met?"

"I cannot see how," he said. "Surely I'd recall being introduced to so fair a flower as you."

"You're too kind, sir. But you seem familiar, somehow. Still, I cannot place . . ."

She gasped, remembering. Cauldon's was the voice she had heard discussing the British plans for Bunker's Hill. His boot had splashed water on her as she hid beneath the tavern step. Now she was seeing him face to face.

"Is something wrong?" he said.

"No," she said. "Only that . . . I've just remembered . . . oh dear, do forgive me, Major, but I just realized that my neighbor has a . . . a dog named Cauldon. How very funny."

Richards' eyes widened with horror. Marsten roared.

"Cauldon, you hellhound," he said, whacking the major's back, "she's got you pegged well enough. Was the dog named for you, or were you named for the dog?"

"I could not say which would be less flattering," Cauldon said, straightening his tunic. "But I do hope I can dance better than a hound at any rate. Miss Jennifer, will you honor me?"

"If the captain doesn't mind."

"Not at all," Richards said. "You'll save the next dance for me, won't you, Miss Jennifer?"

"Certainly."

Cauldon escorted her to the drawing room, where they joined two lines dancing a minuet. Unlike his fellow officers, who were already boisterous with drink, Cauldon remained poised and polished—too polished, she thought. His steps, his turns, his bows all seemed exercises in perfection rather than pleasure. Dances should be fun, she thought, a revelry of manners in motion, with generous doses of humor thrown in for inevitable mistakes. Reducing a dance to ribaldry, as many in the room were doing, demeaned it. But encrusting it with meticulous deliberation robbed it of its joy. Cauldon moved efficiently, flawlessly, purposefully, like one pressing a military campaign to a strategic objective. The only lapse in his performance was his eyes. They never left her and seemed to feast insatiably on her features. Even when she looked away, she could feel his steady gaze on her cheeks, her neck, her tresses.

"Something to eat?" Cauldon said when the music finished.

"If you wish it."

He led her to the dining room and piled high a platter of food for her. From a passing tray he lifted a glass of punch, and in the parlor he shooed two junior officers from their chairs.

"I'd like very much to learn more about you," he said, sitting beside her.

"Won't you eat something first?" she said.

"In your company I lose all my appetite, Miss Jennifer. Tell me more about yourself."

"There's little to say."

"Nonsense. A girl of your abilities and charms . . ."

"What do you know of my abilities and charms, Major?"

" 'Tis obvious you're intelligent with strong opinions and convictions, unimpressed by pretense or shallow gestures."

"Try the mutton," she said. "It is delicious, and the punch is so very sweet."

"Only the best. You say you've just arrived in Boston?"

"From Philadelphia. Goodness, where do you suppose Sarah has gotten to?"

"I'm sure Styles is taking good care of her."

"She's quite a charmer, is she not?"

"Not half so charming as her sister."

"This is the best meal I've had since coming to Boston," she said. "It seems a century ago we tasted any decent fare."

"I do hope our dreary conditions won't chase you back to Philadelphia."

"My father doesn't expect to remain long in Boston."

"I hope I can persuade him differently. Tell me, where do you lodge? I'll have a word with him."

"I'd rather you didn't."

"Ah! They're playing a cotillion. Shall we dance it together, Miss Jennifer?"

"I've hardly finished my food."

"We can come back to it. Or would you prefer a walk in the back garden? It is quite beautiful—first rate."

"A cotillion would be fine, thank you."

She set aside her plate and returned on his arm to the drawing room. After the cotillion they danced a quadrille.

"And now, Major," she said, "if you will please excuse me, I must see how Capt. Richards fares."

"You can't be leaving me just yet," he said. "The evening's hardly begun."

"But I promised the captain—"

"We are just getting to know one another, you and I. I should be very glad if you would—"

"Major," she said, "my promises may mean nothing to you, but they are everything to me. I assured Captain Richards of a dance, and he shall have it."

"I meant no offense, Miss Jennifer," he said with a bow, "I've just . . . well, I confess that I find you entrancing. You're witty, intelligent, obviously well-bred and very beautiful besides. You can't blame me for wanting all of your attention."

"You flatter me too much, Major. It makes me doubt your sincerity. But do take pity on poor Captain Richards. After all, 'twas he who invited me. Look at him, sulking so. It pains my heart."

"Aye," Cauldon said. "On our next skirmish I must arrange to put him in the front ranks and see that he's killed."

"You cannot mean that."

"A jest, Miss Jennifer, I assure you."

"But even to think such a thing . . ."

"I'm a soldier, trained to recognize threats and eliminate them."

"Is Capt. Richards a threat?"

"Only if he harbors affections for you."

"I am not a fortress to be taken, Major."

"A thousand apologies, Miss Jennifer. My professional mind carries me away too easily. You're quite right, of course. Go, satisfy the lad's craving for your company. But do hurry back."

"Unless I find his attentions more tenacious than yours, sir."

She crossed the room to Richards, who chatted glumly with several officers.

"Capt. Richards," she said, tapping his shoulder, "you promised me a dance, and up to now you have left me disappointed."

He turned, stunned to see her offering a hand to him.

"I do beg your pardon, Miss Jennifer," he said, spilling his drink. "It is just that . . . I didn't mean to be rude, really."

"I forgive you. Will you gentlemen excuse us, please?"

"Certainly, miss, by all means."

"How wonderful of you to remember me," he said as she strolled on his arm to the drawing room.

"You've been very patient," she said. "It has taken me quite a while to escape the major. And I still have a plate of food in the parlor. Perhaps you can help me finish it."

"Gladly, Miss Jennifer."

His pleasure was short-lived. Halfway through the dance Cauldon appeared at his side.

"Do you mind, Richards?" he said.

"Certainly not, sir."

The captain retreated to the wall.

"I couldn't bear to be away from you another minute," Cauldon said as he took Rachel's hand.

"Your lack of self-control does you little credit, sir."

"Are flowers despised for craving sunlight? Does the night sky not long for the moon's glow?"

"I am a woman, Major, not a lantern. I have a mind and will of my own, which may not coincide with yours."

"All the more reason for me to admire you."

The music ceased, and the dancers exchanged bows and curtsies.

"With you on my arm, Miss Jennifer," Cauldon said, "every turn ends too quickly. Are you still hungry? We've plenty of fare remaining in the dining room."

"There you are, sister," Sarah said, snagging Rachel's arm. Officers trailed her across the room.

"You'll have a glass of punch, won't you, Miss Sarah?" one said. "These crumpets are wonderful. Won't you try one?"

"More plum pudding, Miss Sarah?" said another.

"Goodness," she said, "what kind of Christmas goose am I that you try to fatten me so? Josephine, dear, will you sit with me for the comedy?"

"Jennifer," Rachel said through clenched teeth.

"Aye, Jennifer, of course, how silly of me. These gentlemen say the play's to be shown in the garden. Are there any gardens left in Boston?"

"Ours is most handsome, Miss Sarah," Styles said, worming his way to her side. "Do allow me to show you."

"Is the program as comical as everyone says?"

"I fear it will be far less amusing than the farce playing out in Philadelphia."

"La, sir," she said, swatting his arm. "Whatever do you mean?"

"Only today I heard the most ridiculous tidings."

"Styles, you have news?" Marsten said. Officers crowded the captain.

"Of the first order, sir," Styles said. "That band of miscreants who call themselves a congress have declared this Boston rabble the Continental Army."

"Fancy that," Marsten said. "How did you learn of it?"

"I was in Gage's office this morning," Styles said. "A host of dispatches arrived from Philadelphia aboard the *Vulture.*"

"Well, speak up, man, what's the word?"

"With one stroke of a pen," Styles said, "the rebel congress has created the largest, most fearsome fighting force in the world. Not only that, they've appointed a new commander-in-chief as well."

"Who is he?"

"Haven't the foggiest, but he's on his way to Boston now—a veteran of the French and Indian War, I'm told."

"One of ours? Impossible. The fool will be leading only cannon fodder."

"If you regard them such a trifle," Rachel said, "why do you not venture forth and conquer them before he arrives?"

"Because they've twenty-five thousand men under arms to our three thousand," Styles said. "Whenever we form up against them, they melt into a thousand households."

"So you sit here doing nothing," she said.

" 'Tis not my decision to make, I assure you. At present, Gage hasn't the stomach for much more."

"But sir," she said, "if this new commander-in-chief should organize them into a real army . . ."

"He shan't, lass. They're mongrels, nothing more. They've got no head for obeying orders, nor the wit to employ genuine tactics. I've yet to see any courage among them. In the face of a real fight, they run for the woods."

"Thus far the strategy has served them well."

"There are ways we could bring them to battle," Cauldon said from across the room. He sat by an open window, swirling his glass and toying with the tassel on his sword hilt.

"Do tell us, Major," Rachel said. "How do three thousand regulars whip twenty-five thousand rabid hounds?"

"Aye, tell us, great sage," Marsten said, "what is your battle plan?"

"Hear, hear," the officers said. "Go on, Major, tell us."

Cauldon rose to his feet.

"Like it or not," he said, "the girl's right. We should take the offensive and finish them before their new commander arrives."

"He shan't make a decent thing of them, I tell you," said Marsten. "I'll wager a bottle of port on it."

"How daring of you, Maj. Marsten, when Gage is wagering all our lives on it."

"I say Gage is correct, Cauldon. A garrison as small as ours is useless against so vast a mob. What's needed to subdue this people are large armies. If we must, we should hire foreign troops to assist us."

"Whom shall we hire, Maj. Marsten, the French?"

"His majesty is kin to the German folk. They may be sympathetic to our cause."

"Tell me if you can," Cauldon said, "how long we'll take raising such an army. One year? Two? And why should the German people assist us in taming our own colonies?"

"What say you then, Cauldon? How should the king's men-at-arms prosecute this war?"

Cauldon drained his glass.

"We slouch behind our Boston ramparts," he said, "bemoaning the deplorable state of our fighting forces and fearing the growing strength of the rebels. I say their strength is an illusion. They're as ravaged by disorder and disease as we. They have no powder, no ammunition, no supplies, no command structure, no order of battle. 'Tis true they outnumber us, but we can harass their flanks and rear. We could even employ our ships to bombard them from the rivers and fire the coastal towns that supply them."

"How can you be certain the rebels are so distressed?"

"Were we energetic enough to scout across the river," Cauldon said, "we might know for a fact. As it is, we busy ourselves at comedies."

"Without adequate forces," Marsten said, "your suggestion is reckless and foolhardy."

"When is warfare not reckless and foolhardy, Maj. Marsten? We've opportunities aplenty to confound the enemy, but no one loftier than a private will listen to me."

"Oh, sir," Rachel said, "do tell us more of your ideas."

"Look here, fellows," Cauldon said. "We have among us a girl who's more interested in military matters than the king's own officers."

"I've no head at all for such things," she said. "But I do like a good intrigue."

"Cauldon, you're wasting your time," Marsten said. "Whatever it is you're planning, you'll have little chance to carry it off. Gage has you chasing a different sort of foe."

Cauldon groaned. Other officers laughed.

"Major," Rachel said, "your chore cannot be so demeaning as that."

"I fear it is," he said. "I'm to ferret out the renegade phantom called Regina Silsby."

Sarah coughed up her punch.

"The ghost?" she said. "Has she been seen?"

"Just before the battle on Bunker's Hill."

"Did you hear, sister?" Sarah said, tugging Rachel's sleeve. "How thrilling."

"Incredible," Rachel said.

"She intrigues you, does she?" Cauldon said. "Gage believes her a bad omen for us."

"Do you think we shall see her again?" Sarah said.

"I'm ordered to see her swinging from a gallows before I may do anything else."

He gulped more drink and called out, "Who knows aught of this ghost, Regina Silsby? Is she as hideous as everyone says?"

Ladies gasped and retreated to the walls.

"Upon my word," Cauldon said. "One would think I had just conjured up the very devil."

"You mustn't speak her name," said a pale girl in a pink gown. "She will think you are calling her, and she will come."

"In that case, she'll save me the trouble of finding her. Why does she frighten you so?"

The girl turned away, hiding her face in her fan.

"Come now," Cauldon said, "there must be someone among us who can enlighten me."

89

"Sir," said a young lieutenant, "I've a private in my company who claims to have seen her."

"Fetch him," Cauldon said. "Let us all hear of this unholy terror, Regina Silsby."

"Your servant, sir," the lieutenant said. "I'll send for him directly."

He left the room.

"Steward, my glass is empty," Cauldon said. "More drink, all around. Let us fortify ourselves against the horrors to come."

In silence the officers gulped their beverages, refilled their glasses, and drank again. Minutes passed before the lieutenant returned with a nervous private. The soldier's weathered face was burned by the sun, his hands mottled, his fingers thick and gnarled. Gray hair protruded from the black tricorn atop his head. He stood stiffly before Cauldon.

"What's your name?" Cauldon said.

"Yates, sir."

"How long have you been in his majesty's service?"

"Twenty-two years, sir."

"French and Indian War?"

"I was in the assault on Quebec, sir."

"Scaled the cliffs, did you?"

"Aye, sir."

"Were you with us at Bunker's Hill?"

"Front and center, sir. In the thickest part of it I was, sir. Same at Lexington and Concord."

"So, you're no stranger to the terrors of war, are you, Yates?"

"No, sir."

"They tell me you've seen the ghost, Regina Silsby."

Yates gaped at Cauldon.

"Answer me," Cauldon said. "Is it so?"

"Aye, sir, 'tis so, sir," he said, quivering and staring straight ahead. Sweat formed on his brow.

"What can you tell us of her?"

"A witch's ghost, sir."

"As ugly as everyone says?"

"Worse, sir. A rotted corpse she be, with flesh so decayed it falls off her bones. 'Twas nigh to a year ago I saw her, and I pray God I never see her again. She took possession of a young woman at the time—a shipmaster's daughter—and stole away to the grave with her."

"A young woman?"

"The ghost needs living flesh to stay earthbound, sir, that's what I'm told. She robs a hapless soul of her body and keeps it till it rots apart. Then she's up from her grave a-looking for another one. They say she seeks a husband to join her in the grave, so no one's safe from her evils. When I beheld her, she was just about rotted apart, and still she was strong as an ox and quick as a cat."

Women whitened. Sarah clutched her throat.

"A shipmaster's daughter, you say?" Cauldon said.

"Aye, sir. A beautiful, God-fearing lass she was, so goes the tale. But then that ghost got hold of her. Possessed her, body and soul. Afore long she was brewing vile potions in her father's house and bathing herself in them for protection against her evil spells. Folks say she bewitched her entire household and doomed them all to perdition. She was to be

91

hanged for her sorceries, but on the morning of her execution she conjured up fires from hell and burned away the scaffold, sir. Then she fled across the harbor. Walked straight upon the waters, she did, and vanished in the fog. There was a captain in Col. Leslie's regiment tasked to hunt her down, same as you, sir. On the very day she vanished, he went stark raving mad. No one could explain it. An earl's son, he was, sir."

Silence choked the gathering.

"Well," Cauldon said, "it seems my task is more formidable than I first suspected. A corpse, you say?"

"Dead as she can be, sir, so there's no stopping her. Musket balls pass straight through her, and fire harms her not at all. If you was to hang her, she'd merely let her head drop off her shoulders and continue on without it."

"I see. Well, thank you, Yates, that is all."

The soldier saluted and left. Cauldon gazed about the room.

"Come now," he said, "why so dour? Surely you don't believe these silly superstitions?"

"Regina Silsby's up from her grave," said a pallid woman, "and none of us is safe."

92

Nine

❦

A Carriage Ride

Abruptly the party ended. Women refused to linger after hearing Regina Silsby's name, and their escorting officers were obliged to take them home.

"Styles, Richards," Cauldon said as the two captains whisked Rachel and Sarah to their carriage, "I shall ride with you. There's a matter I wish to discuss."

Chagrined at having him along, Rachel crammed herself in a forward corner of the coach. To her relief Richards managed to sit beside her. Cauldon took the seat opposite with Sarah and Styles.

"How dreadful," Sarah said, clinging to Styles's arm. "Did you see how terrified that man was? He looked nearly undone."

" 'Twas unnerving, even for me," Richards said. "The fellow's seen more horrors in battle than most of us, yet the mere mention of Regina Silsby's name turns his bowels to jelly."

"Can we not change the topic?" Rachel said. "Maj. Cauldon, what is so urgent that it cannot wait until the morrow?"

"Actually, Miss Jennifer," he said, " 'Twas you that's given me a splendid idea for confounding the rebels. 'Twill be a bold undertaking, unlike anything we've ever done. I'm wagering these two gentlemen are up to it."

"Thank you, sir," they said.

"Do tell us," Rachel said.

"I don't wish to bore you, Miss Jennifer. The captains and I shall have a chat after we've seen you safely home."

"You shan't bore me at all. Quite the contrary, I should be enthralled to hear birthed a spectacular military endeavor."

"Now it is you who flatter me, Miss Jennifer."

"I'm sorry, Major. I do hope your modesty is not from a lack of confidence."

"Make no mistake, Miss Jennifer. I am most confident."

He leaned back and let his eyes drift beyond the window. Rachel watched him, wondering how to goad from him his plan. Without doubt he was energetic enough to follow through on whatever he was scheming. Absorbed in thought, he gazed at the passing houses without seeing them, his brow furrowed, his fist thumping his chin.

"Here we are," Richards said when the carriage rolled to a stop. "Dock Square. Do let us see you to your door, ladies."

"We'd be so grateful," Sarah said.

"No," Rachel said. "Father would be in fits. The square is close enough."

"But the ghost," Sarah said. "You heard what that fellow said. She'll steal our bodies from us and doom our souls to hell. We'll be cursed to wander the earth for eternity, as she does. Oh, it makes me shudder."

"From what I'm told," Rachel said, "we're no safer in our rooms than in the streets. And what good would these gentlemen do us? One wave of her hand would send them all to Hades."

"How can you be so cavalier?"

"I belong to God, Sarah, not to the devil."

"Miss Jennifer, you are a remarkable lady," Cauldon said. "You're either very brave or very reckless."

"No more than you, Major. I choose not to have my actions hampered by a silly demon. Come, Sarah. 'Tis time we were abed."

Richards descended to the pavement.

"Good night, Miss Jennifer, Miss Sarah," he said, assisting the girls to the ground. "I wish you would reconsider."

"Thank you, Captain," Rachel said, "for a most entertaining evening."

"I am sorry it ended so poorly," he said. "Perhaps we may meet again."

"Perhaps."

"If you could give me an address where I may call upon you . . ."

"You needn't concern yourself about finding me," she said. "I'm sure we shall see each other again."

"Until that happy moment, I'll hover about Dock Square like a . . . well, I was going to say *like a ghost*, but under the circumstances . . ."

"Like an angel, then," Rachel said.

"Just so, like a protecting angel. Thank you so much, Miss Jennifer. A very good night to you."

He kissed her hand.

"And to you, Captain," she said. "Maj. Cauldon, Capt. Styles, fare you well. Come along, sister."

She took Sarah's arm and tugged her down the lane.

"Why wouldn't you let them see us home?" Sarah said.

"Because they will badger us day and night with their courting."

"Is that so bad?"

"What sort of patriot are you, Sarah? You cheer the rebels to victory and flirt all the while with their enemies."

"They are fine fellows, those three. And don't tell me you didn't think Capt. Richards charming. He was certainly smitten by you."

"As long as he wears a red uniform, we shan't find much common ground between us."

A dog growled. Sarah squealed and flung herself into Rachel's arms.

"For heaven's sake," Rachel said, prying herself loose. " 'Twill be your own noise that draws Regina Silsby to us. See here, we've arrived already at our own doorstep, and not a single phantom has confronted us."

" 'Tis luck and nothing more."

They climbed the stairs to their chamber. Sarah pitched several logs into the hearth and fanned the embers to flames.

"Light those candles by the bed there," she said. "I'll do the sconces."

"I must visit the privy," Rachel said while tugging on her darkest skirt.

"How can you think about going outdoors with Regina Silsby lurking about?"

"What has come upon you, Sarah? Until now you were eager to see her."

"No more. The circuit riders made her sound heroic, but that poor fellow says she's ghastly. I've never seen a man so frightened. And the other women—they were petrified."

"Superstitious hens."

"What do you know? You've never seen her. That wretched private has. Oh, Rachel, I'm afraid."

"Sarah, I've no time for this. I really must go—please."

"Why are you lacing on your boots?"

"The stable yard is filthy. I don't want to dirty my feet."

"I shall go with you."

"No, stay here."

"Not for a minute."

"Sarah, do be sensible. Will you stand alone in the garden while I occupy the privy? 'Tis darker than pitch out there."

"I shall bring a candle."

"Which will snuff out at the smallest breeze. Sarah, you're more likely to meet Regina Silsby outside than here."

"In the carriage you said it matters not at all where we are, indoors or out."

"Aye, but now you have the fire blazing and the room well lit. I'm sure she shan't disturb you in all this light."

"Even so, I'll not leave your side."

"If you must have a companion, seek out Grandfather or old Col. Dowd. The colonel will be glad of your company."

"What sort of protection could he afford?"

" 'Tis better than being sucked under the sod by Regina Silsby. Go and find the colonel, Sarah. I shall be straight back."

After grabbing her cloak, Rachel fled the room and descended the stairs. By the time she reached the garden gate, she was hooded and masked. With her skirts clutched to her waist, she raced down the lane and across Dock Square. Sounds of clopping hooves echoed in a street beyond, and she followed them to the next crossroads. Ahead of her the carriage rolled over the cobbles. She sprinted after it, grabbed the iron scrollwork between the wheels and leapt onto the vacant footman's bench.

Through the open window drifted a hushed conversation. She raised an ear to the portal, but the din of hooves and carriage wheels swallowed the words. Higher still she lifted her head, praying she would not be seen.

"We shall crush them pocket by pocket," Cauldon said. He was huddled with Styles and Richards inside the coach.

"All that's needed," he said, "is to get some of our fellows onto the mainland dressed as the rebels are, without uniforms or insignias, and lightly armed. We'll deploy them in bands of a dozen or so, fighting as the rebels do, striking and vanishing away again."

"Our men are not trained for such tactics," Richards said.

"If we gathered the cleverest from our various companies and drilled them secretly, we could see it through."

"Aye, sir, but if they are caught by the rebels, they'll be hanged as spies."

"Fortunes of war, Richards. Disease is killing our men in dozens now. If we must die, let it be while fighting. I should prefer that to wasting away on a hospital pallet."

"But sir," Styles said, "Gen. Gage has you chasing Regina Silsby."

"That's the beauty of it," Cauldon said. "In the name of hunting the ghost I may do whatever I want, go wherever I please. I shall concoct all manner of places she's been seen. We shall traipse out after her and wreak havoc as we go. The longer she eludes us, the more mischief we shall make. We may even see our terrors blamed on her. She'll become odious to the rebels."

"A brilliant ploy, sir," Styles said.

"Our first chore," Cauldon said, "is to kill this new general of theirs."

"Sir," Richards said, "you're not serious."

"Am I not? We shall decapitate their army before it has a chance to form. Styles, did the dispatches identify him or state when he's expected?"

"They did name him, sir, but please forgive me, I cannot recall it."

"You said he was a veteran of the French and Indian War."

"Quite a distinguished one, so I understand. He's a Virginian. The documents were dated the middle of the month, so he may arrive any day now."

"Have we any informants on the mainland?"

"None that I'm aware of, sir."

"We'll need a spy among the rebels straightaway. I want to know the moment he arrives. Once he's killed, we shall begin ambushing their camps one at a time."

"Begging your pardon, sir," Richards said, "but is not such a plan . . . beneath us?"

"What do you mean?"

"Your proposal, sir, if I may speak candidly, sounds to me coarse and brutal. 'Tisn't fighting at all, merely murder."

"Is it less murderous to stand in ranks and blast each other to oblivion?" Cauldon said. "Killing is killing, Richards. By finishing their commander-in-chief, we'll spare the lives of every man in uniform and the lives of many provincials as well, for whatever that's worth."

"Sir, the rebels are but a rabble. Left alone they may eventually start killing each other."

"Unless they starve us to death first. Rabble or not, that pretty wench is right. Twice we underestimated these poltroons and paid dearly for it. Our method of fighting will not work against them; we've seen as much. Therefore, we must use their own methods to defeat them. And we must start straightaway, before their new commander can assert himself. That's my plan, gentlemen. What say you?"

"You may count on me, sir," Styles said.

"And you, Richards? Are you with us?"

The captain opened his mouth to reply, but no sound emerged. He stared through the carriage's rear window, his face frozen in shock. Cauldon followed his gaze. Leering through the opening was a ghastly skull flecked with rotting skin. Its sunken eyes gleamed with fiendish fire, and the tangled mouth stretched into a grimace. Instinctively he recoiled.

A scream boiled in his bowels that he struggled to contain. By the time he'd mastered his terror, the ghoul was gone.

"Driver, stop," he said. "Stop, I say, at once."

The coach skidded to a halt.

"Did you see that?" Richards said.

"What?" Styles said, looking about. "I saw nothing."

"Regina Silsby, you idiot," Cauldon said. "She was in the window there. Fall out. We must find her."

They tumbled from the carriage.

"She can't have gone far," Cauldon said, drawing his sword. "Hang me if she didn't hear every word we said."

"But how could she—"

"Don't ask questions, man. Find her. Driver, did you see anything?"

"Sorry, sir. I was watching the road."

"She'll ruin everything if she escapes. Styles, search the alley there. Richards, you take the lane. I'll go this way. If you come upon her, kill her."

"But sir, she's . . . she's a . . ."

"She's what, Richards?"

"Aye, sir, right away, sir."

Cauldon dashed beyond the coach. With his blade he probed niches, doorsteps, rubbish heaps, his ears alert to every sound. He searched empty rain barrels and tipped wooden benches. Even the flower boxes he tickled with his sharpened steel. Cats fled from him; rodents scampered into crevices. From an alley lunged a snarling dog.

"Out of my way, mongrel," he said. He lanced the animal and left it dying. Venturing into the dark passage, he heard a thump, then a grunt. The sound was close by. Slowly he surveyed the shadows. Behind him a whip cracked.

"Styles, Richards," he said, bounding to the street. The carriage rumbled toward him. Atop the driver's box sat the phantom, her bony claws flailing the lash and reins. Her face, barely visible in the halo of the running lamps, was a withered mass of decay. Eyes like two fiery pinpricks glimmered inside her shriveled head.

Cauldon's legs refused to move. At full gallop the horses charged him, their iron shoes sparking on the pavement. At last he managed to leap aside. The carriage hurtled past him. Styles and Richards emerged from the alleys.

"After her," Cauldon said as the carriage veered around a corner. By the time he reached the crossroads, the coach was gone.

"Blast," he said, hammering his sword hilt on a barrel.

"Sir," Styles said, "if we follow the sound, we may yet catch her."

"Right. Hurry on, then."

They ran along the street, pausing at every crossroads to gauge the coach's progress. Soon the noise ricocheted from several lanes at once.

"This way," Styles said, pointing up the hill.

"No, she's heading for the waterfront," Cauldon said.

" 'Tis an echo you're hearing, sir. She's this way."

"We'll separate. You two go that way, I'll go this way."

"Sir, it might be better if we—"

"No time to argue," Cauldon said. "Get your carcasses moving."

He left them dashing up the hill while he descended to the harbor. The clamor faded from him. With a curse he realized Styles was right. But no, the noise was returning. Wheels and hooves clattered toward him, then shifted to a lane opposite. The sound bounced from house to house, reverberating through the maze of streets. He spun about, uncertain which direction to run. Suddenly the clatter assaulted him from two places at once. One was an echo, but which?

The carriage appeared directly ahead of him, its driver's box empty. Cauldon leapt onto a doorstep as the coach thundered by.

"Styles, Richards," he yelled. No answer. Out of the gloom ran the night watchman, his lantern swinging on a long pike.

"Have you seen her?" Cauldon said.

"Who?"

"The ghost, Regina Silsby."

"Can't say I have. There's a runaway carriage—"

"She was driving it."

" 'Twas she, then," the watchman said. "In the square she stopped and turned the team around, then dismounted and sent them galloping this way. I called after her, but . . ."

"You chase the carriage. I'll pursue the ghost."

"Well enough. She's on her way to Fish Street."

Styles and Richards appeared.

"We spied the carriage, sir," they said, panting. "She wasn't on it."

"Come with me," Cauldon said.

"Wait," said the watchman. "Where's the coach headed?"

"Cornhill, toward Marlbrough Street," Styles said. He and Richards followed Cauldon along the waterfront. At a tavern doorway they collided with several subalterns.

"The ghost is out," he said. "Rouse your men. Form search parties at once. I want every house along Fish Street checked, understood?"

"Aye, sir."

"Major," Styles said, "yonder is a fleeing cape. If that's the ghost, she's doubled back."

"Take two men and follow after her. Richards, come along with me."

Rachel banged through the back gate of the Hawkins house. She had hoped her pursuers would follow the empty carriage, but somehow they had seen through her ploy. Still, she was not as exhausted as they, having ridden the coach for most of her journey. In the tangled alleys she had out-distanced them.

Above the house's covered terrace shone Sarah's window, bright as a beacon. The other rooms were dark. Had Sarah taken company with the colonel? If not, the room beside hers was vacant, and its window was open. Rachel straddled a corner rain barrel and climbed a garden trellis to the roof. No sooner had she crouched on the cedar shingles than a pair of soldiers stumbled into the stable yard. Both carried swords.

"I'm sure I saw her come through here," said one. She pressed herself against the slope. It was slippery with moss, and she dared not stir.

"Check the stable. I'll search the larder."

"Hold. Look there."

Something bustled in the lane beyond the fence. Both soldiers exited by the gate, and their footsteps soon tramped the back alley. She crept along the roof and squeezed through the open window.

The chamber was dark and silent. With a relieved sigh she closed the sash and spread the curtains over the glass. As she reached to strip off her hood, a sharp click stopped her.

"Don't move," said a woman's voice. Rachel turned toward the sound, her heart thumping. A lantern opened. Sarah leaned against the bed's headboard, her quaking hand clutching a pistol.

"I know who you are," she said. "You're Regina Silsby."

"That is what I am called," Rachel said in her frog's voice.

"What do you want?"

"You wished to see me, Sarah Gooding."

"How do you know my name?"

"I know much about you," Rachel said. "I know that you should be in the next room, and not in this one."

"I expected you to come there looking for me, so I hid here."

"You've been too clever for both of us."

Sarah adjusted her grip on the gun.

"They say musket balls pass through you," she said.

"If that be so, your pistol will do you little good. Put it down."

"Don't move, Regina Silsby, or I'll shoot. My father taught me to use firearms, and I shan't miss you at this distance. You've come to steal my body from me, haven't you?"

"Mine suits me well enough. Why should I want yours?"

Soldiers crowded the stable yard. A fist hammered the tavern door.

"Open," someone shouted.

"If you haven't come to possess me," Sarah said, "why are you here?"

Rachel had no time for explanations. She heaved a sigh and said in her own voice, "Because I'm sharing the bed with you."

Sarah's jaw fell open. Before she could speak, a knock rattled the chamber door. Grandfather stepped into the room.

"There's soldiers downstairs," he said, closing the panel. "What in heaven's name are you doing in here? You've got the wrong chamber."

He gaped at the ghost, then at Sarah.

"Am I interrupting something?" he said.

"I've captured Regina Silsby," Sarah said. "She's come to terrify me."

"Has she, now?"

Footsteps pounded the lower hall. Grandfather bolted shut the door.

"Well done, Sarah," he said. "Let's have a look at her, shall we? Put up your pistol, lass; you're liable to hurt someone with it. Don't fret; you're safe enough. There's a good girl. Now then, Regina Silsby, will you kindly peel away that ugly face for us?"

The ghoul dropped her hood. Boots thumped the stairs as she stripped off her tattered wig, exposing a scalp of scarred leather. Sarah's eyes widened. The ghost loosened the laces behind her neck. At last she stripped away her ragged skin.

"Rachel!" Sarah said.

A fist pounded the door.

"Open," said a gruff voice, "in the name of the king."

Ten

Secrets

"Open this door at once, or I shall break it in."

"Quick, Rachel, Sarah," Grandfather said. "To bed with the both of you, straightaway. You've been asleep since your party, understood?"

Rachel peeled off her cloak and gloves and stuffed them under the bed sheets.

"Would someone please explain to me—" Sarah said.

"No time for stories now, lass," Grandfather said. "We must see to the soldiers first."

Rachel dove between the linens.

"Sarah, get you down," she said. "I'll tell all later."

"But—"

"Unless you want to see me hanging on a gallows, you'll feign a deep sleep. Please, Sarah, don't betray me."

Sarah blinked her confusion, then buried herself in the bed. Moments later she was snoring. Again the fist pounded the door.

"Open, do you hear?" said the voice.

"Aye, hold your horses," Grandfather said as he shuffled toward the entry. He mussed his hair and unbuttoned his waistcoat before sliding back the bolt. Two soldiers burst into the room.

"Get you dressed and fetch yourselves downstairs," said a lieutenant in the hall.

"Goodness," Sarah said with a yawn. "Is that you, Father?"

She rubbed her eyes and squinted at the soldiers. The lieutenant gasped.

"Miss Sarah," he said. "I'm terribly sorry to disturb you so."

"Bless my soul," she said, shielding her eyes from his lantern. "I know you, do I not? You're . . . dear me, let me think."

"Greeves," he said, embarrassed. "We talked earlier this week, in front of the State House. You were sitting with your sister."

"Aye, certainly," she said. "Why are you barging in on us?"

"Humblest apologies, Miss Sarah," he said. "Captain's orders. We're to turn out the entire household."

"Whatever for?"

"Regina Silsby's been seen. She may be in this very dwelling."

"The ghost? Gracious me! Rachel, did you hear? Wake up, Rachel. Mercy, she sleeps more deeply than a dead woman. Rachel, do wake up. Regina Silsby's close by."

Rachel shrugged away Sarah's prodding fingers.

"Rachel, up with you now, come along. We've company present."

"Tell them to go away and come back on the morrow."

"You may tell them yourself, if you like."

Rachel rolled onto her back. Her eyes fell on the soldiers, and she screamed.

"What are they doing here?" she said, bunching the bed sheets to her throat. "I am in my nightshirt."

"They say the ghost is in the house."

"What ghost?"

"Regina Silsby, of course. Have you seen her?"

"I've been asleep."

"And I," Sarah said. "Bad luck. I should like very much to meet a real ghost."

"Miss Sarah, you're in great danger," said the lieutenant.

"Mr. Greeves, there's been no one here all night but we three," she said. "Surely you aren't mistaking one of us for a corpse, are you? Wait, don't answer that until I've had a chance to fix my hair. The only place Regina Silsby could possibly hide is in the wardrobe there. Be a dear and check it for us, would you?"

He yanked open the closet and exposed its empty innards.

"There, you see?" she said. "Not a single ghost in sight."

"Even so," he said, "I've got my orders. Everyone's to be turned out on the double. I'm dreadfully sorry, Miss Sarah, but you'll have to show yourselves in the sitting room."

"Will you grant us a moment to dress?"

"Aye, certainly. We shall wait for you downstairs."

He retreated with his soldiers to the hall, and Grandfather latched the door. Rachel swung her booted feet from the bed.

"Mercy, Rachel, you've muddied the sheets," Sarah said. Rachel shoved her mask and wig into a pocket and rearranged her hair behind her head.

"You'd better change your dress," Grandfather told her. "Someone may recognize it."

"All my clothes are in the next room."

"We'll have to fetch them somehow."

From the window he scanned the stable yard. It was teeming with soldiers.

"There's no going across the roof," he said. "The corridor's our only chance."

He cracked open the door and peered into the hall.

"What in heaven's name is the meaning of this intrusion?" came a bellow beyond the doorway. Col. Dowd blocked the passage with his nightshirted frame.

"A thousand pardons, Colonel, sir," Greeves said, saluting. "The captain's ordered us to turn out the household."

"Why, for pity's sake?"

"Regina Silsby's been seen. The captain thinks she came through this very house. Everyone's to be searched, sir."

"Including these two girls? Outrageous, man. Is your captain's order a proper excuse for disturbing young women in the middle of the night? I won't have it, do you hear? Anyone can see they know nothing of this."

"Of course not, sir. I was merely obeying—"

"Tell me your name and company."

"Greeves, sir, fifth regiment."

"I shall speak with your superiors in the morning, Lieutenant Greeves. Now be about your business. I shall vouch safe for the ladies."

"Aye, sir. Thank you, sir."

The lieutenant descended the stairs.

"Please accept my apologies, Miss Sarah, Miss Rachel," Dowd said with a bow. "I do hope you'll permit me to make up for the bad manners of our men."

"They are merely following orders, Colonel," Rachel said, "like the fine soldiers they are."

"Nonsense. A king's officer must exercise good judgment in the performance of his duties."

"Lieutenant Greeves has not inconvenienced us too much, Colonel. A bit of sleep is all we've lost."

"Even so, I would make amends for his rude behavior. I insist on your joining me for some refreshment."

"You are too generous, Colonel, but Sarah and I are not properly dressed, and if I may be bold enough to observe, neither are you."

" 'Twill take but a moment to remedy."

"Another evening we shall be much better company. Sarah and I will make ourselves especially pretty for you, and you must wear for us your grandest uniform."

"Tomorrow?" he said. "Supper?"

"We shall look forward to it," she said, extending her hand to him. "Thank you, Colonel, for defending us so nobly."

"Don't go just yet," he said while kissing her fingers. "I've a gift for you and Miss Sarah, if you'll just give me a moment."

He disappeared into his room and emerged with a kettle of steaming milk.

" 'Tis hard to come by," he said, "but a colonel's rank has its privileges. This will put you to slumbering before the next quarter-hour strikes."

"Gracious," Rachel said. "Thank you so very much, Colonel. We shall have it immediately. Good night."

"A very good night to you, my dear."

She retreated with the kettle to their own room, and Grandfather latched shut the door.

"Well," he said, filling a tin mug, "the old colonel appears to be good for something after all."

"Enough chatter," Sarah said. "You promised to tell me what has happened just now."

"Talk in whispers," Rachel said.

"Well enough. What's going on here?"

"You told us you wanted to see Regina Silsby, did you not?"

"Aye."

Rachel reached into her pocket and fished out the leather mask.

"Here she is."

Sarah stared at the mottled hide. Two eyeholes were blackened with soot, and strips of shorn leather formed a mangled mouth. A gash laced with leather ties split the entire back of the skull.

"Do you mean," Sarah said, "that you . . ."

"Not so loud."

"Are you saying that *you* are Regina Silsby?"

Rachel nodded.

"And you've been terrifying all of Boston with . . . with this?"

Again she nodded.

"I cannot believe it."

" 'Tis gospel truth."

Sarah looked to Grandfather, who bobbed his head. She dropped onto the bed and stared at the ragged leather.

"Why did you not tell me?" she said. Grandfather stuffed tobacco into his pipe.

"We couldn't risk anyone knowing," he said. "My father always told me, 'If you would keep a secret from your enemy, tell it not to your friend.' After we fled Boston last year, we feared Rachel's whereabouts might become known to the redcoats. That's why we never mentioned her escapades to you and why we never sent word to Robert."

"The stories are true, then," Sarah said, "in a manner of speaking. You are the shipmaster's daughter possessed by the ghost. And your entire family vanished away with you."

"Never to be heard from again," Rachel said. She laughed at the silliness of it.

"What of those vile potions they said you were brewing?"

"I was washing in my father's barn."

"Why is that so terrible?"

"I was washing myself," she said.

"Do you mean you were bathing? Deliberately getting yourself all wet?"

"It is wonderful, Sarah. You must try it."

"Never. I shall lose my life by it."

" 'Twas a hot bath that saved mine."

"How do you manage to change your voice like that?"

"I swallow the words into the back of my throat."

"Goodness, Rachel, I could be a ghost myself. Do let me go a'haunting with you. Let's go tonight."

"It is not for sport, Sarah. The idea is not to be seen at all. Besides, we haven't any reason to go romping about just now."

"We've reasons aplenty. There's redcoats to confound and . . . I know! Let us steal the gunpowder at Portsmouth. Don't look so shocked, Rachel. I learned of it from Col. Dowd while you were out. He's quite talkative, actually. We could fetch it to the rebels."

"Or get ourselves killed. Sarah, you don't even have a mask."

"We shall fashion one for me."

"How will we transport the powder? The kegs will weigh a hundred pounds each. Or do you expect the soldiers to help us? 'Excuse me, good sir, but may I beg your assistance with these heavy kegs of gunpowder? And would you be kind enough to escort us past the fortress gate?' Really, Sarah, you must think it through first."

"I want to do something. 'Tisn't fair, you bounding all about Boston while I gather weeds. And I think it awfully rude of you not to share your secret with me. You never even told your brother where you were. Now you've lost him. He may be dead for all we know."

"Lasses, 'tis not a safe place to talk," Grandfather said.

"Indeed," Rachel said. "Sarah, come along. We're going out."

"This very minute?"

"Why not?"

"The soldiers . . ."

"They're gone, or did you not notice?"

Sarah peered into the stable yard. It was deserted.

"Upon my word," she said.

"If you're to be a ghost," Rachel said, "you'll have to pay better attention to your surroundings than that."

Sarah bounced up.

"And so I shall," she said, grabbing her shawl. "Where are we bound?"

"Come and see."

Eleven

❧

The Grave

The cemetery gate screeched open.

"We're going in there?" Sarah said, trembling. "Without a lantern?"

She clutched her shawl to her shoulders and peeked through the iron bars. Tombstones speared the uncut sod. A breeze stirred the trees.

"Come," Rachel said, stepping into the graveyard.

"Not I. That place is foul with evil spirits."

"Then we'll not be pestered by anyone living. Hurry, before someone sees you."

"I've changed my mind. I wish to go home."

"Don't be such a coward, Sarah. Come along."

"Why can we not visit on the morrow?"

"In the daylight we will be seen. Follow after me. I've something to show you."

"I don't like this, Rachel. 'Twill be the death of us."

"I already told you that Regina Silsby is not a ghost."

"And if you're wrong? Suppose she's lurking among those trees—the real Regina Silsby, I mean. She may be angered that you have defamed her. If we trespass on her grave . . ."

Rachel grabbed Sarah's wrist and pulled her past the gate. The portal banged shut.

"There, we're safe inside," Rachel said. "That wasn't so bad, was it? Come along, this way."

She waded into the tall grass.

"Rachel, don't leave me."

"Follow along."

Sarah glanced over her shoulder to the distant street lanterns.

"I do wish we had a lamp," she said. "Let's go back for a candle. Rachel, what say you?"

Her cousin was already lost in the cemetery darkness.

"Rachel, wait for me," Sarah said. She pushed through the weeds and struck her knee on a granite marker. With a cry she clutched her leg.

"Hush," Rachel said, appearing at her side. "Mind your step."

Sarah glanced downward and saw her shoe sinking into a burial mound. With a yelp she jumped aside.

"Will you please be quiet," Rachel said.

"I was standing on top of someone."

"I'm sure he didn't mind."

"What if I've offended him? He'll reach up through the earth and—"

"For heaven's sake, Sarah, they're all gone to God."

"Or to the devil."

"Either way, they're not here. We've nothing but discarded bones and dust beneath us. Come along."

"Rachel, take my hand."

"Very well."

They wandered through the shadows. Headstones were randomly arranged in pairs and clusters. Some stood alone. There were granite slabs, timber crosses, planks rudely carved. Tree roots had cracked and crumbled many markers. A few had rotted away or disintegrated into rubble, and the names they had borne were forever lost.

"There she lies," Rachel said, halting at an arched stone beneath a tree. " 'Twas here my adventure began."

Sarah studied the granite. In the moonlight she could barely read its epitaph.

Here lies ye
body of
Regina Silsby

aged 21
departed this life
Nouem 15, 1742

None but ye heart
knows its sorrow
and none can
share its joy

"She was Grandfather's sister," Rachel said.

"For a fact?"

"A more godly woman never walked the earth. 'Tis a shame I should be the one to soil her reputation so."

She told Sarah about the Boston Tea Party, when British soldiers had chased her to the very spot on which they stood. In the darkness they had mistaken her for a phantom and fled. She described making her goblin's disguise and using it to save her brother from arrest. Next she recounted the grounding of the *HMS Devonshire,* her escape from the gallows, and her family's flight to Philadelphia.

"To you," Rachel said, finishing her story. "No one else knows the tale."

"I envy you."

"Why?"

"Such an exhilarating adventure. My life is dismal in comparison."

"I would greatly prefer a placid life."

"While those of us condemned to tedium crave a fiery escapade."

"That's the problem with adventure," Rachel said. "We spend all our time wishing for it, and when it finally comes we're thrown into such a panic that we wish it were quickly gone. Then we tell everyone how thrilling it was."

"But life without adventure is dreary," Sarah said. "How miserable we would be if every day plodded to a dull, inevitable conclusion. I don't wish to live that way, and I daresay you don't either. We'd be no better than cows munching grass in a field."

"I never thought of that. Mercy, Sarah, you're quite right. 'Tis the unexpected that gives the day its spice. Some seasonings are sweet, and some are sour."

"And the best meals offer both. One flavor heightens the other."

"But if we're made to love excitement so," Rachel said, "why does St. Paul admonish us to lead peaceful and quiet lives, as is pleasing to God?"

"Perhaps we are to find peace in the midst of our adventures," Sarah said, "to savor the quiet and the calamity together."

Rachel pondered her words.

"I never considered life a banquet," she said, "but it is exactly that. God is setting before us a feast filled with sweet and savory dishes. Some of us favor the bland foods . . ."

". . . you, for instance . . ."

". . . while others gobble everything in sight . . ."

"I beg your pardon."

"On some occasions we're forced to eat things we don't want, and other times we're deprived of dishes we crave. And most often we desire whichever is not in front of us. How foolish we are."

She knelt beside the grave.

"What are you doing?" Sarah said.

"I wish to pray."

"Must you always be praying? Really, Rachel, you should join a convent. Night and day you bow your head at the slightest provocation. Your lips move, but no sound comes out, as if you were talking to the dead. Most times you don't even close your eyes. 'Tis frightening the way you pray. Why must you always be crying out to God?"

"Apart from Him our lives are meaningless and confused."

"Even *with* Him our lives are meaningless and confused," Sarah said. "I see not how He changes anything, be He near or far."

"He is never far from any of us. 'Tis we who are far from Him."

Sarah heaved an irritated sigh.

"Very well," she said, kneeling beside her cousin. "If you must, pray for both of us."

She bowed her head, clamped shut her eyes, and tucked her fingers to her chin. Rachel watched her, amused, and lifted her hands to heaven.

"Dearest Father," she said, "what a delightful discovery we've made just now. How good of You to—"

"Mercy, Rachel, do you really expect Him to answer a prayer like that? 'Dearest Father, how good of You . . .' Do you not realize whom you're addressing? He is the king of the universe, not some doddering parent."

"How do people address your father?"

"They call him 'Mr. Gooding,' or 'Merchant Gooding.' But I don't see how that has anything to do with—"

"How do you address him?"

"I call him 'Papa,' of course. What else would I call him?"

"And were he the king of England, would you not still call him 'Papa?' God is our Father, Sarah, not some faraway monarch. Why should we not call Him 'Father,' or even

'Papa?' Just now I've made a happy discovery. I want to sit in His lap and tell Him about it."

"How do you propose to do that? He is spirit; you are flesh. For heaven's sake, Rachel, you can't even see Him. He's probably off beyond the stars somewhere. I don't know how a peasant girl like you can expect to approach a king so lofty as He, especially after calling upon Him so casually."

"You don't know Him very well, do you?"

"I know Him well enough to address Him properly."

"But I am the one praying just now, so if you'll permit me . . ."

Sarah folded her hands and clamped shut her eyes.

"I pray He doesn't strike us dead for our irreverence," she said.

"Father in heaven," Rachel said, "I have been a fool. All this time I've been complaining about the tempest swirling about me. I expected to find my brother straightaway, but instead we are swallowed in a maelstrom. In my heart I have been grumbling about it ever since. I want things to be easy; I want them to go as I expect them. But just now You've shown me I really don't want that at all."

"He didn't show you," Sarah said, "I showed you."

"The words were yours, but the thought behind them was His."

" 'Twas my own thought, if you don't mind."

"May I continue? Lord God, forgive me for desiring what I don't have and disdaining what I do have. When things are quiet, I am bored; and when they're raucous, I am terrified. I see now that one flavors the other, and I should be grateful for both. Help me accept whatever You put before me. You know better than I what is good for me. Help me receive what You provide; help me embrace it. Let me find You in my circumstances and love You through them. I pray too that You will show Yourself near to Sarah. Show her that You are a God close by and not far off."

Footsteps sounded behind them. Sarah yanked a pistol from her waist.

"Whoever you are," she said, "you'll keep your distance, please. We are praying."

"Hold your fire, lass," Grandfather said. "Permission to approach the line."

"Show yourself."

He stepped from the shadows, and she lowered the gun.

"Had I known you take your prayers that seriously," he said, "I'd have left you in peace."

Slowly he eased onto his knees beside them. For a long time he gazed at the mottled stone.

"Told her everything, have you?" he said. Rachel nodded.

"Thirty-three years she's been gone," he said, pressing a hand to the sod, "and hardly a day goes by that I don't miss her. May the good Lord bless you, Reggie."

"Reggie?" Rachel said. "Is that what you called her?"

"Called her many things, I did—Pip, Squirt, Weed, Turnip. Whatever it was that irked her, 'twas that I called her."

"What did she call you?"

"Monkey."

"Whatever for? Did you resemble one as a youth?"

"I once brought home a banana tree from the tropics," he said. "Set it in the parlor by the bay window and ate the fruit when it ripened. Afterwards she always called me 'Monkey.'"

"Sir," Sarah said, "do you think she minds having her name bandied about so profanely?"

"She's with the Lord, lass, and there's not much to trouble her here. Finish your prayers, you two, and then I've got some tidings."

"We are done," Rachel said.

"For the moment," Sarah said.

"I'm told your brother may have joined one of the militia regiments," he said. "That would put him on the mainland shore, somewhere between Dorchester and Chelsea."

"How did you learn this?" Rachel said.

"There's a bookshop over by the Province House. The patriots gather there in secret. I visited while you were out, and one of the lads remembered your brother."

"We must cross over at once," Rachel said.

"But you promised we would go a'haunting," Sarah said. "There's nothing for Regina Silsby to do over there. The enemy is here."

"We came to find my brother, Sarah, not to confound the British."

"I don't see why we cannot do both. There are three of us now."

"Hush, someone's coming," Grandfather said. At the cemetery gate a pair of soldiers peered into the graveyard.

"Follow after me," he said. "We'll leave by the back way."

"How tiresome," Sarah said. "Can we not frighten them first?"

"Look there," said one of the soldiers. "What's that in the cemetery?"

His companion stared through the iron gate.

"A woman?" he said. "I see two . . . no, three persons."

He reached for the latch.

"Hold," said the first, grabbing his comrade's sleeve. "That's Regina Silsby's resting place. Trespass there, and you'll not come out."

"Upon my word, is she the ghost?"

"Aye, with two others at her side. By my faith, they've vanished."

"You don't think she's conjured up other spirits, do you?"

"If she has, we're all worse for it."

Twelve

Letters

Rachel strolled with Sarah and Grandfather along the dusty Cambridge highway. Sarah's glib tongue had gotten them easily through Boston Gate. Fresh Concord grapes were their goal, she had told the guard. Old Col. Dowd had expressed a desire for fruit, and the girls wished to fetch some back for him. No, they didn't have a pass; their gift was meant as a surprise. Would the dear sentry mind letting them through just this once? Her smiles and flatteries had cajoled him beyond compliance, and the trio ambled over Boston Neck without a care.

Breastworks of stone and earth crowded the isthmus, surrounded by spiked fences and deep ditches. The ramparts bristled with cannon and mortar, and flags fluttered above the mounds. Crimson-coated soldiers lined the entrenchments, their weapons trained toward the forests.

Barely a musket shot beyond the Neck sprawled the rebel camps. Like slums they littered the fields and spilled into the woods. Dwellings were squalid patchworks of canvas, timber, turf, and brush. Unshaven, unwashed men crammed every space, their reeking bodies swathed in farmers' frocks, buckskins, and tunics of various cuts and colors. The luckier ones wore boots, shoes, or moccasins; the rest wrapped their feet in rags or went barefooted. Shirts and coats disintegrated on men's backs. Breeches, leggings, and trousers had been patched, repatched, and still were falling apart. Nowhere was a laundry kettle or a soap tub visible. A stench of sweat, filth, and rotten meat permeated the air.

Three drill sergeants bellowed commands in an open field while their slovenly ranks shouldered sticks instead of rifles. For every man exercising, six loafers watched. Two squabbling militia companies fell silent long enough to stare at the girls before resuming their dispute.

Up the south road rattled a carriage drawn by four horses. Mounted men surrounded the coach, liveried in blue tunics, white breeches, and black boots.

"You, get off the road," a swordsman shouted. Grandfather ushered the girls beneath a large chestnut tree.

"What's the fuss?" Rachel said.

"Someone of rank, I should guess," Grandfather said as the carriage rumbled by. "That fellow is either very pompous or very important."

The troop halted at the town house. From the coach stepped a man of remarkable stature and regal bearing. Swaths of gray streaked his auburn hair, which was knotted behind his neck with black silk. A cape of dark blue draped his athletic frame to the knee.

At the town house entry appeared a rotund, aged officer still strapping on his sword. He saluted the newcomer, who returned the courtesy before shaking the fat man's hand.

"General of some sort," Grandfather said.

"Perhaps he's the new commander-in-chief," Rachel said.

"I should think he'd warrant a fancier reception than this."

The two officers disappeared into the house, and the carriage disgorged its remaining passengers.

"Bless my soul," Grandfather said. "That can't be old Jimmy Tims there. Ahoy, mate."

A blue-coated colonel turned toward them. His face lit up.

"Bust my breech buttons," he said. "Henry, you old horse."

He strode to the tree and clapped Grandfather in a boisterous bear hug.

"Fancy finding you here," Tims said.

"I should like to know," Grandfather said, "how a ne'er-do-well like yourself can rise to such prominence. The last time I saw you—"

"Not another word, Henry, or I shall order you horse-whipped. I'm a colonel now, and I can do that sort of thing."

"Who's the big fellow you've arrived with just now?"

"Gen. Washington. He's the newly appointed commander-in-chief. All the way from Virginia he's come."

"Not much of a turnout for him."

"The general wished to arrive quietly. He'll make his presence felt quickly enough. Be sure of that."

"Is he up to the task?"

"Hard to say. The New Englanders wanted one of their own, but the Congress thought it best to appoint someone from the southern colonies. Unity and union, that sort of thing."

"What of his competence? Did the Congress consider that?"

"Oh, he's well qualified—fought under Braddock in the French and Indian War. Saved the command, I'm told. The question is whether the New Englanders will follow him."

"He's got a chore before him."

"Upon my word," Tims said, mopping his brow. "I toured the camp before his arrival. Nothing but anarchy. We've very little by way of supplies, and no long-term volunteers. Most of these regiments signed on for a year's duty, and their time's almost expired. If the general doesn't persuade some to re-enlist, he'll have no army at all."

"Will he manage it?"

"If he does, he's got more powers than Moses. These boys want to go home. Ask any one of them, and they'll tell you they've done more than their share."

"How are you for powder?"

"Not good. There's not a plant in New England that can fashion the stuff. If we're to have any at all, we must cart it up from Philadelphia. At present we've only thirty-seven kegs on hand."

"I'm told there's a fort full in Portsmouth. Perhaps we could fetch it out."

"A fine idea. I shall put it before the general."

"Does he know of the Ticonderoga guns?"

"Aye, he'll want them here straightaway. But without powder they're useless to us."

"Provisions?"

"Only what we can forage from the countryside. We've no stores at all on hand."

"There's ships aplenty in Boston harbor stuffed to the gunwales," Grandfather said. "Just arrived."

"Would that we could get our hands on some of it."

"Perhaps I may barter a service with you."

"What did you have in mind?"

"Have you quill and parchment?"

"In my trunk. They're lifting it off the carriage now."

"Rachel, Sarah," Grandfather said. "Come along. You'll write letters home to your kin while I have a chat with Col. Tims here. Do you mind, Colonel?"

"Your servant, sir. But this cannot be little Rachel. Bless my soul, child, at our last meeting you barely reached my waist. Now look at you, a grown woman. I shouldn't expect you to remember me at all."

"How do you do, Colonel," she said with a curtsey.

"Old Tims sailed with me a time or two," Grandfather said.

"Or two!" Tims said. "Oh, Miss Rachel, the tales I could pour into your ears. We must have supper together."

"Thank you, Colonel," she said. "Allow me to introduce to you my cousin, Sarah Gooding."

"Charmed," he said with a bow. "Ho there, fetch that trunk to the tree here. Aye, you! Bring it here. Hurry on, I haven't got all day. Ladies, I hope you are agreeable to sitting outdoors in the shade. At present I'm not certain where I'll be quartered."

Before the girls could answer, he fit a stout key into the chest and popped open the hasp.

"My trunk is the only writing surface I've got at present," he said while passing parchment, quills, and ink to the girls. "When you're finished, I'll post your letters with the dispatches. Now come along, old man," he said, seizing Grandfather's arm. "Tell me what's boiling in that pea brain of yours."

The girls settled into the grass. Rachel stared at her blank page, tickling her chin with her quill, pondering what she might say. Sarah started scribbling immediately. Nearby a cluster of ragged minutemen gathered.

"There's a sight I've not seen in a while," said one, leaning on his rifle. "How long are you lasses here for?"

"Only until we've completed our letters," Rachel said. "Have you been long with the army?"

"You hear that, lads? She's called us an army."

"Have you not heard?" she said. "The Philadelphia Congress has declared you so."

"Does that make us the Congress's army? We're free men, lass. We take commands from no one. Come December I'm back to my family."

His companions murmured agreement.

"What will become of your liberty," she said, "if no one rises to replace you in the ranks?"

"Haint my concern, missy."

"Until the redcoats arrive to burn your farm, sir. Then you'll have but one shot against a thousand."

"I'll fret about that when the time comes."

"And come it will, if you don't see this through to the end."

"Listen to her, lads; she's a talking handbill. At Lexington and Concord we beat back the redcoats, lass, and we shall do it again."

"Unless they learn from their mistakes," she said. "They brought no cannon to Lexington, and no cavalry. Next time you shall see both. If you quit your chore before it's done, you'll win nothing but the king's ire. I say you're better served if you remain in the army. With your great numbers and your new commander just arrived, you shall drive the redcoats completely from our shores."

"By my faith," the man said. "I'll not be listening to you any more. You'll have me committing to a lifetime of servitude. Come along, lads. Leave this magpie to her letters."

The men shuffled away.

"True sons of liberty," she said.

"At least they've left us alone," Sarah said. "I cannot think with all that chatter."

She dipped her quill and continued scratching her parchment. Rachel watched her. Three months had passed since they had promised to return home with Robert. After so much time the entire household must be wondering if she and Sarah were still alive. She dipped her quill and began to write:

July 2, 1775

Dearest Mother and Father,

I pray this letter finds you well. We enjoy good health and are well taken care of. Our attempts to find Robert are thus far fruitless, but we continue to search. We are told he may be among the militia regiments, so we will look for him there. Please don't fret about us. We are well, but the war has taken its toll on Boston. Few merchant ships remain in the harbor. Many houses are unoccupied and torn down, as are countless barns and fences, all gone for fuel. Most of the trees have also been cut down. Our house still stands as a barracks for cavalry with the horses berthed in our barn. The shutters and the fence have all been stripped away, and the garden is trampled to nothing. It is sad to see our home in such a state. I look forward to the day we may return to it. When chance permits, I shall write again. Until then, with all my love, I remain,

Your obedient daughter,

Rachel

"Finished so quickly?" Sarah said as Rachel blew dry her ink.

"I've said everything I can think of."

Sarah scanned Rachel's delicate script.

"A bit gloomy, are you not?" she said.

"What have you written?"

Sarah showed Rachel her letter.

Greetings and salutations to my own dear Mother and Father,

How thrilling have been these past weeks! Boston is reduced to a most wretched hovel, of course, with the port closed and the patriots besieging the gates. Even so, we're as merry as can be. Already Rachel and I have attended a ball and danced with many dashing officers. The fare was far better than the rubbish available to common folk.

You'll be amazed to know that Regina Silsby has again shown her face! Only last night the ghost followed after a trio of scheming redcoat officers who discovered her riding the back of their carriage! A wild chase about town ensued, during *which the ghost swept into our own house like a whirlwind, even invading my own bedchamber. I saw her with my own eyes! She's ghastly. Her skin is tangled rot that drops from her face in chunks, and she smells like a rubbish heap. Her eyes are firebrands that burn through your very soul, and her arms and hands are nothing but bones. She spoke to me with a voice like gravel and even called me by name. I tried to protect myself with a pistol, but she vanished away as quickly as she appeared, leaving me unharmed. I slept badly after that and still shudder at the thought of her hideous face. I fear I may never sleep again.*

"Are you not exaggerating things a bit?" Rachel said.

"Aye, that's the fun of it."

Rachel scanned her meager lines.

"Sometimes I wish I were more like you," she said. "You're so spirited, so lively."

Sarah laughed.

"I want to be more like you," she said.

"Why?"

"You're solid as granite, Rachel. Even with a pistol shoved in your face you're unshakable. Sometimes I think myself more flighty than a cork bobbing on the ocean. I wish I had half your courage and daring."

"It is easily gained."

"How?"

"Rachel," Grandfather said, marching toward them. "Finish your letters, and get you up at once. We've a little chore to do."

Thirteen

Diversions

"Your job is to create a respectable distraction," Grandfather told Rachel. He stood with her and Sarah on a bluff
overlooking the Charles River.

"Old Tims has given me thirty-six men experienced at
sea," he said. "We'll be taking captive those three supply
ships yonder. Tomorrow night after the ten o'clock chimes,
you and Sarah will make a disturbance ashore while we slip
up the far gunwales and surprise them. We'll be away to Salem or Marblehead before anyone realizes."

"Where shall we meet again?" Rachel said.

"Cambridge at the Vassal house. Col. Tims has seen to
your quarters there. I'll be a week or so bringing the stores to
the rebel encampments."

"So be it," Rachel said. "A distraction you shall have."

"Make it a big one," he said. "We can't risk failure."

"It shall be done."

"You and Sarah will be going back to Boston by your-selves," he said. "Take care, and look to Col. Dowd for your protection. He's a silly old fool, but he'll pull rank where you're concerned."

"A guardian angel he shall be to us," Rachel said.

"Very well then. I've much to do, so I'll not be seeing you again until our raid's done. Tims has assigned a guard to see you safely beyond the rebel lines. After that, you're on your own."

"We shall manage," Rachel said. Grandfather placed his hands on the girls.

"Go with God," he said. "The Lord bless you and keep you safe."

"Amen."

He led them back to Cambridge, where Tims stood wait-ing at the town house.

"All set to go?" he said.

"As ready as we'll be," Grandfather said.

"I've arranged for the ladies to travel with Dr. Morris. He's a king's man, attached to the fifth regiment."

"A redcoat physician?" Rachel said. "Why is he here?"

"The medical profession knows no allegiance, lass," Tims said. "Our own physicians have been tending the British wounded as well. Sergeant, where's your detail?"

"Three riflemen plus myself ready and waiting, sir, as you ordered."

"These are the ladies I spoke of," Tims said. "The doctor has agreed to bring them into Boston."

"Aye, sir."

Grandfather hugged both girls.

"Take care," he said. "Look to Col. Dowd."

"Don't you worry about these lasses," said the sergeant. "We'll see them safe and sound to the British ramparts. Now where's that Dr. Morris gone to? Ah, there he be. Ho, Doctor, we're ready to march. These here are the ladies joining us."

A lean man approached the group, his face bronzed by the sun. Dark wool covered his frame, and a queue of gray hair hung beneath his tricornered hat. On his back was a canvas pack. He carried a leather satchel in one hand, a walking stick in the other.

"By my faith," he said, smiling broadly. "Heaven has certainly favored us today, Sergeant. Do permit me to introduce myself, ladies. I am Dr. William Morris, surgeon to his majesty's fifth regiment."

"We are Sarah and Jennifer Gooding," Rachel said. "You're very kind to escort us, Doctor."

"A pleasure, Miss Jennifer. Sisters are you? Where in Boston are you lodged?"

"Near Dock Square," Rachel said.

"I'll see you safely there. Sergeant, lead on."

"Very good, sir."

They started down the road.

"How does a British physician come to be in the rebel camps?" Rachel said.

"A privilege of my profession," he said. "I offered my assistance to Col. Prescott, and he accepted."

"What is your estimation of the rebel conditions?"

"Dreadful," he said, "and most of it their own fault. The men seem loathe to feed themselves properly. They won't wash their clothing, let alone their bodies. Meals are nothing but red meat, and drink is all liquor. I've yet to see a company dig a proper privy. And you can't make a single man listen. Time and again I've warned them of the risks they run, but there's no one who can issue an order they'll obey. This love of liberty will be the death of them."

"From what we've seen," Rachel said, "the king's forces are hardly better off."

"True enough," he said. "Scurvy and smallpox are ruining us, and we're hard pressed for decent provisions."

"What of the supply ships recently arrived?"

"The officers are seeing to themselves first, arrogant fools. I'm told that privateers as far south as the Carolinas have begun raiding our shipping. Between their piracy and the sea's perils, we'll be fortunate to receive half of the provisions sent us. Most of that will rot before it arrives. But enough of this gloom. The day's fair, the countryside is pretty, and the company most agreeable. What errand has brought such charming ladies to the rebel camps?"

"Oh," Rachel said, "we were . . . let me see, we were . . ."

". . . visiting our uncle," Sarah said.

"Aye," Rachel said. "After the rebels overran the country, he feared for our safety, so he lodged us in town until the trouble passes. We do miss him very much."

"You may be home with him before too long," the doctor said. "Unless those rebels add vegetables to their diet and take pains to remove their wastes, the entire mass of them will die before the winter. Our own forces will suffer the same fate if we don't fetch some fresh provisions to them. This entire affair may end by an act of God."

"How did we fall to such a state?" Rachel said.

"I think these rebels a most surly and ungrateful lot," he said. "Nothing but a drunken, canting, lying, praying, hypocritical rabble. The very doctrines of liberty that caused their rebellion make them disregard their own officers. And why not? Men cannot bear to be commanded by their equals. Without distinctions of birth, fortune, and education, no social structure can stand. These fellows think to undo precedents of civilization set for hundreds of years."

"Perhaps the rebels see it differently," Rachel said.

"How so, my dear?"

"I have read their pamphlets, and—"

"How very enterprising of you."

"—they say that under kingly rule, rights and privileges seem only to apply to the king and his favorites. If I am a lord and you are a peasant, I may do to you what I will without restraint because the king's grace rests on me rather than on you."

"It is his right," the doctor said, "as ruler of the land. With the responsibilities of government come certain privileges."

"But Christian teaching demands otherwise," she said. "The rebels will tell you that Moses' law forbids men, and thus men's governments, from shedding innocent blood, from restricting worship of God, and from coveting or stealing other men's goods. Therefore, they say, it is God Almighty who endows all men with a right to life, liberty, and property.

140

This precedent dates back to the Exodus from Egypt and is established by God Himself."

"Go on."

"Also in Moses' law is the principle to love one's neighbor as one's self."

"But no government can force men to love one another," he said.

"Aye, but governments can enforce the principle."

"How so?"

"By seeing that all men are treated equally before the law. There is no partiality with God, so wrote St. James in his epistle. God's law is based on the rights of individual men, not on the rights of kings. By that argument kings and their agents should not be treated differently before the law. If a peasant steals, he is brought before the magistrates. If a nobleman steals, he must face the same magistrates and suffer the same penalty as the commoner. The rebels say that the law is king, not the other way round."

"You are remarkably well read for a woman," Morris said, "especially for one so young and pretty."

"But don't you see what that implies?" she said. "All people are subject to the same law, from the lowest stable hand to the highest lord. Government, they say, must exist not for the pleasure of one man, or one class of men, but for the protection, safety, and prosperity of all."

"And who sets the laws?"

"God already has, in Moses' commandments. All proper laws must derive from there."

"Does this principle of life, liberty, and property apply to all races and creeds?"

"To Jew and Gentile alike. In Christ there is neither Jew nor Greek, neither slave nor free, neither male nor female. All are equal before God, and thus all must be equal before the law."

"But many of the patriots are slaveholders."

"They shall have to give it up, or show themselves hypocrites."

"Does that also mean that women may become owners of property?"

"I suppose it does."

"Well," he said, "you almost make me want to believe such a paradise is possible."

"Why should it not be? Must America have a king and an aristocracy simply because Britain has one? The rebels say that royalty is a path to corruption, enslavement, destitution, and death. History seems to agree from the Egyptians to the Carthaginians to the Romans and onward. The only safe law is God's law, and the only just government is one that recognizes all people's rights as granted by God. King George has already demonstrated his disregard of them and his preference for a favored few."

"Dear me," said the doctor, "I would almost believe you to be a rebel yourself, Miss Jennifer."

"I confess that such ideals are enticing."

"But how can these lofty sentiments apply to that rabble we've just left? Do you consider any of them to be so nobly endowed? Would you entrust your governance to them?"

"It is true that many of them are pigs," she said. "But we are all sinners, Doctor. The only difference between the rebel pigs and the king's pigs is the cost and care of their attire. But you'll find many noble minds and spirits among the rebels, and many dogs among the king's noblemen."

"Even so," Morris said, "I shall always be convinced that men are sheep, and as such they shall forever need a shepherd."

"And you, Doctor, are you a sheep or a shepherd?"

"Well, indeed, I should think that . . ."

"By your reckoning you are one or the other, and I don't see any trappings of nobility draped about your neck. By the same token, what makes the king or his noblemen proper shepherds? Is it superior ability, or profound wisdom, or merely birthright? If the latter, any oaf may become shepherd to men better than he. Do you not think that a terrible injustice?"

"It is divine appointment that grants a king his rank."

"As determined by the happenstance of his birth?"

"Just so. The lot is cast into the lap, but its every decision is from the Lord."

"And all attempts to better one's lot without the king's permission are sinful?"

"I should think so."

"And that," Rachel said, "is the nature of the contest. The king says 'yea' to arbitrary law and oppression of common folk; the rebel says 'nay'. The rest of us must choose sides and fight it out in a trial by combat. How very medieval. We're like two knights tilting on a green."

"And to the victor go the spoils," said the doctor. "God shows His favor by granting victory to His champion. What a grand epic you've described, Miss Jennifer."

"You mock me, sir."

"Not at all. 'Tis a magnificent pageant unfolding before us, and only God knows its outcome. Why, bless my soul, here we are approaching the ramparts already. Sergeant, I suppose you'll be wanting to return to the safety of your own lines."

" 'Tis about time for us to take our leave of you, Doctor," the sergeant said, touching a finger to his cap. "Them redcoats'll be shooting at us afore long."

"Then I shall thank you for your escort, sir, and bid you farewell."

"Thank'ee, Doctor, for your service to us. And you, lass," the sergeant said with a wink, "you should be buying yourself a printing press."

The militiamen waved their good byes and turned toward the afternoon sun. In the doctor's company the girls easily passed the fortifications and the town gate. All the way to Dock Square he walked them.

"You're certain you won't allow me to see you to your door?" he said.

"We can make our own way from here, Doctor, thank you," Rachel said.

"As you wish. I do hope we may make acquaintance again. Your company has made a dreary journey most enjoyable."

"You do us honor, sir," Rachel said. "A very good day to you."

"And to you, Miss Jennifer, Miss Sarah."

He bowed and left them waving their kerchiefs after him.

"How funny," Sarah said as they bustled along Fish Street. "If the good doctor only knew."

"What?"

"All afternoon he's been escorting the most fearsome fiend in Boston."

"Hush, Sarah. Don't discuss such things. Anyone could hear us."

"Where shall we do our plotting?"

"Let us stroll over to Beacon Hill. On our way back we'll pray in the King's Chapel."

"Again you want to pray?"

"And talk. With our heads bowed no one will suspect a thing. Ah, here's the Hawkins house. Come upstairs with me."

They hurried through the entry, mounted the stair to their bedchamber, and locked the door.

"Try this on," Rachel said, digging into Grandfather's trunk and tossing his mask to Sarah. She fit the leather over her head and tucked the wrinkled folds beneath her blouse.

"Gracious, how uncomfortable," she said. " 'Tis all rough and scratchy in here. I suppose I shall have to get used to it, unless I can find some silk to sew in as a lining. Aye, that's a fine idea. Am I pretty enough to be Regina Silsby's sister?"

"You look as if you were burned to death. At night you'll be even more hideous."

"You're too kind. How shall we find a wig for me? I don't wish to run about bald."

"We haven't time for a wig," Rachel said. "Besides, you look worse without it. Have you a pair of black gloves?"

"In my duffel."

"Let's cut this apron into strips and stitch them on for bones."

They spent an hour altering the gloves, then descended the stair for their stroll. From the kitchen Rachel borrowed a pair of butcher knives.

"What will you do with those?" Sarah said. Rachel hefted a blade, then slung it across the chamber. The steel tip split a gingerbread mold on the hearth.

"I shall think of something," she said.

"How did you learn that?"

"I taught myself."

"Can you teach me?"

"Certainly."

On Beacon Hill they discussed possibilities for a respectable diversion. Rachel described her haunting of the King's Chapel the previous year. They agreed a similar escapade would be grand.

"Look there," Sarah said, pointing down the far side of the hill. "What a strange exercise."

Twelve soldiers were stripped to their shirtsleeves and running a racecourse of obstacles. Strapped to their backs were knapsacks and long rifles. They leapt walls, crawled under fences, vaulted gullies, shinnied trees, climbed ropes, and pulled themselves onto rooftops. At intervals the men tugged free their firearms, dropped to their bellies, and blasted straw dummies standing in a corner of the field. Immediately they leapt to their feet, charged their targets, and assaulted them with tomahawks.

"It is Maj. Cauldon," Rachel said.

"There are Styles and Richards with him," Sarah said. "Whatever are they doing? It doesn't seem at all like a proper drill."

"I don't much like the look of it," Rachel said. "See there; who's that?"

A uniformed officer approached the training field. Cauldon peeled away from his troops and joined the newcomer.

"It is Dr. Morris," Rachel said. Sarah shielded her eyes and squinted at the distant figures.

"He's a spy, Rachel. I'll wager he's telling the major of Gen. Washington's arrival."

"How very clever," Rachel said. "The doctor makes a great show of humanitarian care for his enemies, and they let him wander all about their camp."

"He certainly fooled us."

"But we have fooled him as well."

Fourteen

Assassins

Under a moonless sky the King's Chapel chimed ten o'clock. Rachel and Sarah huddled in the church's graveyard, hooded and masked. Each girl carried a pistol at her waist, and Rachel's pocket bulged with her two kitchen knives.

Intently the girls watched a solitary sanctuary window brightened by candlelight. There the sextant waited for the bell ringers to descend the steeple stairs. The chimes would remain silent until dawn.

"Look there," Sarah said, gripping Rachel's arm. A dozen men skirted the cemetery, their backpacks sprouting long rifles.

"We've been found out," Sarah said.

"Stay calm. Be ready to run."

The men trotted down the hill toward the Back Bay.

"Styles, Richards, this way," said a man at the base of the slope. "Hurry on. I've two skiffs waiting at the Beacon Street pier."

"Mercy," Rachel said, "it is Maj. Cauldon. He must be heading for the mainland."

"To kill Gen. Washington? Rachel, we must follow after him at once."

"But Grandfather's expecting a diversion."

"There are empty houses aplenty," Sarah said. "Set one afire."

"We can't do that."

"Why not? They're all being stripped apart for fuel as it is. Fire one of them, and let us be gone. The entire garrison will come running."

"And half the town may burn," Rachel said. "There must be a better way."

"We haven't time to think of one."

"Hush, Sarah. Yonder come the bell ringers."

Boys spilled from the sanctuary. Behind them hobbled the sextant. He locked the chapel door and limped away, leaving the youths loitering on the columned portico.

"I've an idea," Rachel said. "Come with me."

"What will you do?"

"Follow along and see."

The girls emerged from the cemetery and darted toward the chapel colonnade.

"I dare you," said a stout fellow to one of his scrawnier companions. "Take this knife and stab it into her grave."

"I'll not do it," said the lad. "She'll reach up and drag me under the earth with her."

"Afraid, are you?" the bully said. "Only last night, at the stroke of midnight, I stole up to her tombstone and stuck this very blade through the sod. Felt it tickle her ribs, I did. If you think yourself a better man, you do the same. I'll teach you not to show me up in front of the sextant again. Go on; be a man. Accept my challenge, or be branded a coward the rest of your days."

He pressed his knife into the lad's hand. Rachel grabbed the brute's collar and spun him around.

"Who is this that defiles my resting place?" she said in her toad's voice. "Was it you that pricked my finger, boy?"

The youth shrieked. His comrades cringed against the chapel doors.

"Regina Silsby," he said, crumbling before her. "I didn't do it, I swear. 'Twas only to impress the lads I said it. Never once did I soil your grave."

"For disturbing my slumber," she said, "you shall do a proper penance. If you fail, my sister and I will visit you some night."

"You . . . you have a sister?"

"Yonder, and she is more foul than I."

The boys eyed the hooded ghoul hovering in the shadows.

"Do my bidding," Rachel said, "or taste my wrath. Understood?"

Heads bobbed.

"Go back into the chapel," she said, "and ring every bell in the steeple."

"Ring the bells?" said a lad. "We'll be caned for certain."

150

" 'Twill go much worse if you don't," she said. "Ring them until the magistrates drag you screaming from the tower. Tell anyone who asks that Regina Silsby commanded it. And you," she said, pressing a bony finger to the bully's brow. "Play the organ for me. I would hear its music."

"But I don't know how. I've never—"

"Silence, fool. Get this imp to pump the bellows. You shall release every stop and work the keys. Make as much sound as you can. I would hear it in my tomb. If I am not satisfied, I shall return with my sister to plague you."

"But the doors are locked. We cannot get back inside."

She took her pistol and bashed out a windowpane.

"Now it is open," she said. "Inside with you."

The boys gawked at one another, then scrambled for the opening.

"Remember," she said as each one disappeared through the window, "my sister and I are watching you."

The last lad squeezed into the sanctuary. Echoes of their stampeding feet ascended the tower.

"Jolly good fun, that," Sarah said.

"Come along; we've no time to waste."

"The Back Bay?"

"We must find ourselves a boat."

They raced along Beacon Street. The steeple bell tolled, and lesser chimes started a clanging cacophony. Tuneless warbling spilled from the organ pipes. Townsfolk hurried up the hill, and torchlight soon surrounded the sanctuary. From the waterfront the girls surveyed the rise.

"It resembles a yuletide festival," Sarah said.

"Mind the sentries."

They squeezed into a niche as a soldier wandered by. His gaze was fixed on the chapel summit. The moment he turned a corner, they scampered down the quay.

"There's a fine boat," Rachel said, pointing toward a skiff. She descended a wooden ladder, and Sarah climbed after her.

"Look to the bay," Rachel said as she peeled off the boat's canvas cover. "Do you see the major anywhere?"

"It is too dark," Sarah said, clinging to the ladder. "Hurry on, Rachel; the guard's coming back."

"Don't call me that."

"What shall I call you?"

"Regina Silsby, of course. Stay quiet until he passes by."

"What shall I do if he sees me?"

"Keep still and he won't."

Along the wharf the sentry wandered, still watching the commotion on the hilltop. He crossed Beacon Street, and Rachel resumed her work.

"There, the row locks are set," she said. "Come aboard and loose the bow cable."

Sarah tumbled into the prow and wrestled the burly knot. Finally the rope dropped into the water.

"Shove off," Rachel said. Sarah pushed against the piling. The boat veered from the pier and rolled in the current. Sarah yelped and flailed her arms, almost toppling into the water.

"Quiet," Rachel said. "You'll bring the guard back."

"He's still watching the chapel. We've done it, Rachel; we're away."

"Call me Regina Silsby for heaven's sake. And don't go celebrating just yet. Our journey's hardly begun."

"Look, Rachel, such a grand sight we've left behind us. The chapel seems ablaze atop that hill. And all those strange sounds pouring from it—what a spectacle. I'm sure Grandfather will be very pleased."

"The longer those boys keep at it, the better. Search the waters ahead and tell me which direction to take."

"Where is the mainland?"

"Good heaven's, Sarah, don't you know? A'port is the Charles River. That would be your left as you face forward. Cambridge should be dead ahead."

"Past those warships, you mean. Steer more to the left."

"Are the major's boats anywhere in sight?"

"No, I think they are too far beyond us. Can you not row faster?"

"They've got twelve oarsmen to our one," Rachel said. " 'Tis hardly a fair race."

"Mind that ship ahead. Goodness, such a big one too. How many cannons do you suppose it carries?"

"Guide me past her. Every man aboard will be at the rails looking ashore before long. On the far beam we shan't be seen."

"At this pace Gen. Washington will be dead before we reach shore."

"Put your tongue to better use and pray that he isn't. If you see anything ahead, tell me."

Silently they continued, Rachel grunting with every pull, Sarah guiding her through cutters, brigs, and sloops. Under the spars of a great man-of-war, the boat scudded. The ship's stern windows glowed a dim yellow, and from an open portal drifted jesting and laughter. At the taffrail Rachel saw officers peering toward Boston. She was grateful the moon had not yet risen.

Water slapped the skiff and splashed with each dip of the oars. She wished she had thought to muffle the blades. But no, soggy rags lashed to the sweeps would have doubled their weight and drained her strength further. There was nothing to do but pull.

Beacon Hill's massive bluff slowly vanished astern. The chapel noise died away. Moonlight peeked over the eastern horizon.

"There's the mainland ahead," Sarah said at last.

"Thank God, I'm nearly done."

The boat scraped ashore, and Sarah leapt onto the rocks. Rachel stumbled after her. Together they pulled the boat to the beach.

"Tide's coming in," Rachel said. "Drop the anchor over the side or she won't be here when we come back."

"What difference does it make?" Sarah said. "We shan't be coming back. Our Boston errand's done, and now we're free to follow after the major. With luck he'll be heading to Washington's quarters, the same place we're going."

"Aye," Rachel said, feeling foolish. "Would we had a horse. I'm exhausted."

"We've no time to rest," Sarah said. "Come along, I'll help you."

They climbed the rocks, slipped by the slumbering pickets, and wandered through the woods. At a stone fence on the forest edge they paused.

"Yonder is Cambridge," Sarah said. "I see the Vassal house."

Rachel leaned on the rocks, gasping.

"I must rest," she said. "I cannot take another step."

"Listen, Rachel. Someone's making a fuss."

From the nearby trees came a rustling of leaves and snapping of branches. Voices bellowed and wailed.

" 'Tis a fight," Sarah said. "Are we too late?"

"The general won't be wandering the woods in the dead of night."

"No? Yonder by the fence is a saddled horse."

In the moonlight shone a handsome white stallion with a finely appointed saddle. Rachel's heart quaked.

"Come along," she said, forcing herself toward the sound. Louder and more violent became the disturbance as she and Sarah loped through the trees. Instinctively Rachel tugged free her pistol and checked her pocket for her knives. At a cluster of granite boulders she peered into a clearing surrounded by pines.

To her amazement the noise emanated from a single man. He knelt in a shaft of moonlight, his hands clenched, his face turned toward heaven. Anguish twisted his features.

"Oh God," he wailed, "are these the men You've given me to defend America's liberties? How shall I succeed with such a rabble? What sin have I committed that You thrust this impossible task upon me? Why do You press me so sorely?"

He buried his face in his hands, and then rose and paced the clearing.

"Give me some hope that You have not abandoned us," he said. "Show me what I must do. I am a lost child."

Again he fell to his knees.

"Almighty God," he said, "You need no army to accomplish Your will in this world. What's gathered here is a paltry, pitiful mob. There's hardly a man fit for proper service, and I've nothing to supply those that are. Dear God, show Yourself strong where we are weak. Make us an army worthy of Your name. You are a God who cares for the weak and the infirm. Let all men see that You resist the proud and pour grace on the humble. Breathe life into this noble cause. Fight for us, Lord. Without You we shall surely fail."

Rachel watched him, entranced. Never had she heard a man pray so passionately.

The effectual fervent prayer of a righteous man availeth much . . .

Something disturbed the brush on the far side of the clearing. Sarah gripped Rachel's shoulder and pointed toward the trees. In a thicket Rachel spied a glint of metal. Somehow she perceived a man lifting his rifle for a shot.

"Get down," she said, shoving Sarah to the ground. She thumbed back her pistol's hammer and jerked the trigger. Thunder boomed, and the pistol leapt in her hand. A fireball brightened the thicket, illuminating a startled sniper. His rifle discharged, and his shot went wild. Washington was on his feet a moment later.

"Run, General," Rachel yelled. "They mean to kill you."

Instead he leapt toward the assailant, sword lashing. Into the brush he plunged, swatting aside a rifle, and clobbering its owner on the head. Another rifle barked. Sarah's pistol answered with a flash and a bang. Men came running from across the field. Rachel snatched a knife from her pocket and hurled it at another gunman. He grunted and toppled forward, his rifle erupting as he struck the ground.

"Fall back," Cauldon said from somewhere. Rachel grabbed her remaining knife and scanned the shadows for him. Dark forms retreated from the clearing as minutemen leapt the pasture fence.

"General, are you hurt?" said one.

"Search the woods," Washington said. "Hurry on, before they escape."

"Sir, how many attacked you?"

"I'm not certain. A dozen, perhaps, but there were two who helped me. One was a woman."

"A woman?"

"I heard her call out to me."

"There's not a woman close about for miles, sir."

"I am sure I heard a woman's voice."

"General, sir, we've found two dead over here. Another may be wounded in the woods yonder."

"Find him," Washington said.

"Long rifles," someone said, holding up a fallen weapon. "They've armed themselves as we are."

"But why? There's no reason to attack a lone man in the forest."

They dragged the corpses to the clearing.

"Redcoats, sure enough," one said, "but without uniforms."

Rachel used the distraction to find Sarah. She was pressed against a tree, trembling.

"Rachel," she said, "I think I've shot a man."

"So have I. We must hide, Sarah. Here, among the boulders. No, no, don't climb them. Kneel and cover yourself with your cloak. You'll appear as one of the rocks."

The girls dropped to their knees and crouched side by side beneath their woolen shrouds. Boots crushed the nearby earth as men searched the area. Someone climbed a boulder, stayed a minute, and descended again.

"General, sir, we must get you back to your quarters."

"I would first know who it was that came to my aid."

"He's gone, sir. I beg you return with us to the camp straightaway. More assassins may yet be in the woods."

"Not until I know—"

"Sir, for the good of the army . . . for God's sake, General."

"Very well, Captain."

"Thank you, sir."

The company evacuated the clearing.

"I think they're gone," Sarah said. "Oh, Rachel, what have we done?"

"Stay where you are. The search parties may return. I'll tell you when we may move."

For a long time they huddled under their cloaks. Slowly the buzz of insects returned to the woods. Animals wandered the forest floor. Something waddled to Rachel's side, sniffed her cloak, and scampered away. Her back stiffened, and her knees ached. The air trapped beneath her cloak grew stale. Spasms rattled her chest, and her lungs screamed for air. But far worse was the agony roiling inside her. She had shot a man. Her bullet had struck him, and he had fallen.

Eventually the sound of shuffling boots returned to the clearing.

"Gone," someone said. "Back to camp, most likely. Come along, lads. A fine lot of thanks we got for our troubles."

"Look, sir, there's Haggerty. See if he's had any luck."

A second search party approached the clearing.

"Well, man, what did you find?"

"I think they've all escaped. Devilishly clever, whoever they were."

"Even so, they've done nothing but ruin a good night's sleep for all of us."

"And gotten two of their own killed. I'm off to bed."

"Sir, who do you suppose it was that helped the general?"

"A few of the lads, I expect."

"But he said there was a woman."

"He's daft. When's the last time you saw a woman hereabouts?"

"Yesterday I saw two. Pretty, they were."

"Aye, just the sort to scatter a pack of wolves. Where's your head gone, lad? Get along."

The men climbed the fence and retreated across the field. Rachel scanned the clearing. All was dark and still.

"Come," she said, easing onto her feet. Sarah groaned.

"Rachel," she said, clutching her stomach, "I'm sick."

"Once we're walking you'll feel better. Let's follow the road to the Vassal house."

"I wasn't even thinking, Rachel. That man was about to shoot, and I just lifted my pistol and . . . I killed him, Rachel."

"It couldn't be helped. You saved the general."

"But I shot a man."

"Listen, what's that?"

They stood paralyzed. Something crawled across the ground, grunting and snorting with each movement.

" 'Tis a monster," Sarah said. "It sounds awful. Let us escape while we may."

"No. Follow me."

Rachel circled the rocks and almost tripped over a man lying among the dead leaves. He was pulling himself away from the clearing. A knife handle protruded from his ribs.

" 'Tis one of the assassins," Rachel said. "He's hurt."

She bent over him and touched his arm. He cried out and lay on his side coughing blood.

"You shan't make it to the river," she told him. "We must fetch one of the rebel surgeons at once."

"No," he said.

"But you'll die unless we—"

"Too late," he said. "I'm lost."

"You mustn't say that. Tell me your name."

"Richards. Captain to his majesty's fifth."

"Oh my," she said, pressing a hand to her lips. "Capt. Richards, you mustn't die. Please don't die."

"Your voice," he said between spasms, "do I know you?"

"Hold still," she said, "until we can fetch a surgeon."

"Who are you?"

"A friend."

His eyes rolled upward.

"The stars," he said, "they're so bright tonight. They seem close enough to touch. I wonder . . . if I . . ."

He raised a trembling hand.

"Don't," she said. "Save your strength."

"I hear each one is as bright as our own sun. Do you suppose it is true?"

"I'm sure it is," she said. "Tomorrow you shall see our own sun again. Its warmth will revive you. I shall stay at your side and see that you are well."

"I know you, do I not? You're . . . you're . . . but you can't be."

"Tomorrow I shall tell you. Can you wait until then?"

A shudder ran through him.

"I can't breathe," he said. She held him until his body went limp.

Fifteen

❧

Missing

"He did not deserve to die like that," Rachel said. "That cursed Maj. Cauldon put him up to it."

"So you've said a dozen times," Sarah said. "It won't change anything."

Richards's body had been found the day following the skirmish. He had been buried in the Cambridge churchyard with the other fallen assassins. Rachel dared not attend his grave. Someone might connect her to the mysterious woman Washington had described. Instead she mourned in the solitude of her Vassal house chamber, uncertain why Richards's death had affected her so deeply. He was a redcoat, after all, and he had died while attempting murder. But he had been an unwilling participant in the crime. He had even protested against it. She remembered the night of the comedy, when a single comment from her had pricked his conscience for the better. Such a pliable spirit was rare in a man.

But perhaps Richards had been too pliable. Rather than stand by his convictions, he had let others goad him down a wicked path. The weakness had cost him his life.

"Whoso diggeth a pit," said the proverb, "shall fall therein."

But why had Richards died instead of Cauldon? Why did evil men survive their cruel schemes while good men perished following them? Still, Richards's choice had been his own, and he had paid a terrible price for choosing badly.

No matter how she wrestled the matter, she could not escape a darker truth. Richards was dead because she had killed him. As much as she might wish to blame Cauldon for the tragedy, her own hand had dealt the captain's deathblow.

She had not meant to take his life. Indeed, she had not expected the knife to strike home at all. Her reaction had been instinctive, and she had meant only to ruin his aim. But her intention did not matter. She had killed a good man, and perhaps two. Her own musket ball could well be lodged in another breast buried in the churchyard.

The sun blazed orange in the western sky. For ten days the girls had posted themselves on the bluff overlooking the Marblehead road, watching for the supply train that Grandfather had promised. Sarah passed the time weaving small baskets from blades of grass, picking flowers, writing letters, chasing birds, and reading books supplied by Col. Tims. She cleaned both pistols and reloaded them with cartridges from Grandfather's saddlebag. Rachel prayed for forgiveness, for Grandfather's safe return, for Washington, for the army, for anything else that came to mind. From her perch atop the hill, she watched the warships in the harbor waters and the British fortifications on Boston and Charlestown necks.

"Suppertime," Sarah said as the sun touched the horizon. "We must be getting back before the colonel starts to worry."

"What's taking Grandfather so long?" Rachel said.

"We shan't know until he arrives. There's no use fretting about it."

"Perhaps we should send messengers to Salem and Marblehead. He could be hurt or . . ."

"Let us ask the colonel at supper. He's got as much to gain by Grandfather's return as we."

They gathered their things and descended the hill. Camp inhabitants, accustomed to seeing the girls every day, waved as they passed by.

"Ah, there you are," Tims called from the steps of the Vassal house. "I was about to send for you. Gen. Washington's invited you to dinner."

"Is he not quite busy?" Rachel said.

"Everyone's got to eat, lass. He's seen you atop the bluff, and I've explained why you're there. He wants to meet you."

"But we haven't anything suitable to wear."

"The general's not much for ceremony. I should think him quite happy to see you come as you are."

"At least let us shake out the grass from our dresses," Rachel said, "and put up our hair better."

"Only if you can manage it in two minutes," Tims said. "We're late as it is."

The girls hurried to their chamber and brushed their skirts. After rebundling their tresses, they descended the stairs and met Tims on the front step.

"Perfect," he said, offering an arm to each girl. "You two are about the same age as the general's own daughter."

"Gen. Washington has a daughter?" Rachel said.

"Stepdaughter, actually. She died of a fit two years ago. Patsy was her name."

"I'm so sorry."

"Don't go to despair," he said. "The general's prone to fits of gloom enough as it is."

"I've never been in the company of a general," Sarah said. "I hardly know how to act."

"You needn't waste time with formal compliments and manners," he said. "And for heaven's sake, don't try flattery. Call him 'General' or 'Sir.' Speak sincerely from your heart. He's seen you fretting for your Grandfather, and I think it's got him pining for his own family. You'll do us all a great service if you'll help him forget his burdens for an evening."

"As we must forget ours," Rachel said. They climbed the steps of a large house on Brattle Street. Two sentries allowed them through the front entry, and a steward met them in the hall.

"Col. Tims, sir," he said with a bow, "the general's expecting you."

Through a portal he led them to an elegant parlor, where Washington sat with another officer.

"Ladies," the general said, rising from his chair. "We are delighted you could join us."

He was amazingly tall, his gray eyes glimmering beneath heavy brows. Silver tinted his auburn hair, which was pulled back in a tight queue. A blue uniform covered his frame with a waistcoat and breeches of creamy white. He wore no medals, no decorations or adornments except a pair of gold epaulets on his shoulders. The girls greeted him with curtsies.

"Do allow me to present to you Col. Prescott," Washington said. "Col. Tims you already know."

"A pleasure," Rachel said. "I'm told, Col. Prescott, that you led the patriot forces on Bunker's Hill."

"I wish we could have held it," he said.

" 'Twas a valiant effort, sir. You've shown the world that the redcoat is not invincible. That is a victory of sorts."

"I pray we shall absorb our lessons faster than the British absorb theirs. The fight is hardly over."

"But it is well begun," she said. "General, do I hear correctly that you are from Virginia? Is it pleasant this time of year?"

"Almost as magnificent as Massachusetts," he said. "Now let me see . . . Col. Tims tells me that you are Miss Rachel . . ."

"Your servant, sir."

". . . and this must be your cousin Sarah. I've seen you on the bluff watching for your Grandfather. Is he not the man who raided the British shipping for us?"

"We are not worried about him, really," Rachel said. "In his day he led jaunts far more daring than this last one. Quite an adventurer he was."

"So I'm told," Washington said. "Still is, by the look of things. Miss Rachel, I understand that Boston is your home."

"Until last year," she said. "We fled to Sarah's house in Philadelphia to escape the port closing."

"And why have you returned?"

"My brother is still apprenticed in Boston," she said. "We hoped to bring him away to Philadelphia with us. But since

166

the ruckus at Lexington and Concord, we've lost track of him."

"Quite bold of you to march so glibly into a battleground," he said. "There's much of your grandfather in you, that is plain. What's your brother's name? Perhaps I may assist you."

"Robert Winslow," she said. "Grandfather believes him in one of the militia regiments."

"I shall make some queries," he said. "And I hope we may soon restore your dwelling to you as well."

"My thanks, General."

"Since you're native to Boston," he said, "I wonder if you might answer a question for me."

"I am at your service, sir."

"What you can tell me of this ghost, Regina Silsby?"

Rachel stared at him. Sarah, too, was dumbstruck.

"How do you know of her?" Rachel said.

"Col. Prescott has been telling me all about her. He swears she's the lady who rescued me the other night."

"I'll wager my entire farm on it," Prescott said. " 'Twas she who put me on to the redcoat plans for Bunker's Hill. Stole into my very sleeping chamber and prodded me awake with a pistol. How she got past the sentries I shall never know."

"In the forest," Washington said, "a woman appeared from nowhere. After our little tussle she vanished away just as quickly."

"Did you see her?" Rachel said.

"Not well enough to recognize her again," he said. "All cloaked in black she was, but she was quick with pistol and blade. I thought I saw her face once—unbelievably ghastly."

"She has been known to throw knives," Rachel said. "But how do you know . . . I mean, how can you be sure, General, that it was a woman who helped you?"

"I heard her call out to me. She told me to run—as if I would obey such an order. She was too tall for a boy, and her voice too youthful for a man. But come, you've lived here. What do you know of her?"

"Many in Boston think her a witch straight from hell," she said. "My grandfather believes otherwise."

"Why is that?"

"She was sister to him."

"You don't say."

"By his account she was a saint. She died of a fall on the King's Chapel stairway. Her ghost first appeared on the night of the Boston Tea Party."

"So you believe she is a ghost?"

"I confess, sir, I would have to agree with my grandfather. He says she's gone to God and that some fiendishly clever person is masquerading."

"A right swift person too," Washington said. "Our compatriots in Boston tell us she made a ruckus in the King's Chapel on the very night I was to be murdered. Yet according to Prescott here, she managed somehow to get herself across the river to Cambridge in time to deliver me from my assassins."

" 'Twould require a miracle to manage that," Rachel said.

"Did I hear correctly," Sarah said, "that two ghosts were seen that night?"

"Two?" Prescott said. "Would it were true! That would confound the redcoats sorely. I should be glad to see a whole coven of such ghosts swirling about."

"Her appearance has heartened the men at any rate," Washington said. "To them she's become an omen. God Himself is guarding us."

"Really?" Sarah said. "How grand. Rachel, did you hear?"

"I hardly think we should put all our hope in a ghoul," Rachel said. "General, sir, you can't believe that Regina Silsby is anything more than an ordinary person."

"And I, too, am an ordinary person," he said. "Of such is our entire army made. Does not God Himself employ ordinary persons to accomplish His will? Who knows what may come by the contributions of a single man or woman? I shall never discount any effort for our cause, however small. Great events often turn on a single, insignificant occurrence. Whoever this Regina Silsby is, I pray she never tires of her antics."

"You can be sure of that," Sarah said.

The steward carried a tea tray into the room.

"Ah," Washington said, rising. "Finest English tea, compliments of the Massachusetts militia. I think we may not consider ourselves too traitorous to enjoy a spot."

He filled the porcelain cups himself and offered one to each guest.

"Delicious," Sarah said. "I haven't tasted tea in over a year."

"Do you ladies enjoy games?" he said.

"Very much so, sir," Sarah said. "Have you any favorites?"

"Patsy—my late daughter—enjoyed a few with me," he said. "One of them I packed along. I'm too embarrassed to invite my senior officers to try it, but they may be agreeable if you ladies will join the fray."

"I should like that very much," Sarah said. "Things in Boston are so dreary."

"Come, child," he said. "Mrs. Washington insists we be cheerful whatever our situation. The greater part of our happiness or misery, she says, depends upon our dispositions and not upon our circumstances. I must say I'm inclined to agree. Chin up, Miss Sarah. Face the day nobly, whatever it brings. Find the humor in it, and fix your gaze on that."

"It is difficult at times."

"Agreed, but it must be done."

"Not long ago," she said, "two very elegant Boston gentlemen offered me a dinner of rats. At the time I was repulsed, but on reflection it was rather silly. They were so well dressed, like noblemen, and so proud of their wretched repast."

"Did you taste it?" he asked, amused.

"Heavens, no. 'Twas all I could do to entertain the suggestion."

"Tell the general what you *have* been eating," Rachel said.

"Not on your life," Sarah said. "He would think me no better than a buzzard."

Washington smiled.

"I, too, have had to slop with the scavengers," he said. "Do tell me, Miss Sarah, what is the most dreadful thing you've ever had to swallow?"

"My father's jokes."

"Hah," he laughed. "Very well said. And what of you, Miss Rachel?"

"Let me see . . . I recall one Yuletide my mother prepared for us a very special Christmas goose. She was most secretive about the spices she used and quite proud of the result. I must say it looked succulent, but the moment we sank our teeth into it everyone grimaced. 'Twas the most awful thing ever to cross my tongue. Well, in our household we are quick with compliments and silent with complaints, so the whole lot of us fell quiet as church mice. 'What is wrong?' Mother said, looking about. She popped a fork full into her mouth and promptly spit it out onto the floor. Not even the dog would touch it."

"Marvelous," Prescott said.

"One summer," Tims said, "I was afield hunting with my father. We camped in a dense wood, and in the middle of the night I thought to reach into my pack for a strip of jerky. Imagine my surprise when I grabbed something furry instead. 'Twas the foulest skunk this side of the Atlantic, and it sprayed me with every drop in its sack. No one would come near me for a week. I had to burn all my clothes."

"You don't mean," Sarah said, "that you were romping about . . . oh, dear me."

"We had blankets, of course," he said, "but they were so cumbersome as clothes that I quickly gave them up. Aye, my dear, Adam and Eve were better garbed than I. At the first cabin we sighted, Father went to barter a set of breeches for me. The man must have been bigger than a bull moose, for we could have fit five boys my size into the clothes he supplied us."

"Gen. Washington, sir," said the steward from the doorway.

"What is it, Williams?"

"I thought you might wish to know, sir, that the baggage train from the harbor raid has arrived."

"Come, everyone," Washington said, jumping to his feet, "let us see what our girls' good grandfather has fetched for us. Williams, set another place for dinner."

"Very good, sir."

The general strode to the front steps with his guests tumbling after him. Wagons jammed the road, their timbers sagging under piles of puncheons, casks, and crates. Tethered sheep and oxen crowded the caravan. All along the line militiamen lifted canvas covers and peeked into wagon beds.

"Back," yelled the quartermaster, "back, I say. Sergeant, fetch my clerks straightaway. Have them bring their ledger books. You there, get your hands out of there. Corporal, post a guard until we've had a chance to sort this stuff."

Men ran in all directions, shouting news of the supply train's arrival.

"Well met, sir," Washington said to the lead driver. "What have you brought us?"

"Not as much as we would have liked, General. We got away clean with one ship and took from her what you see before you. There's eggs, butter, cheese, and meal. Powder and shot as well, and some lead ballast we can melt into musket balls."

"There were three ships altogether," Washington said. "What became of the other two?"

"We captured them right quick, sir, but the warships were onto us too fast and cut off their escape. The lads set them afire and abandoned them. They're on the harbor bottom."

"And the men?"

"They got off on the longboats," he said. "Some tried to swim ashore. There was a running fight between the boats and the ships. Our fellows got the worst of it, sir."

Rachel pushed to Washington's side.

"What became of my grandfather?" she said.

"Sorry, lass," the driver said. "His was one of the ships sunk."

Sixteen

※

The Search

"Rachel, you must give it up," Sarah said.

For weeks the girls had wandered Boston's streets, circling every place that might hold prisoners: the Customs House, the Charter House, the State House, Faneuil Hall, Old North Meeting, Old South Meeting, Fort Hill, the empty counting houses along the wharves. At every site Rachel whistled her whippoorwill's cry, pretending to amuse herself with her tuneless chirping, all the while listening intently for a response. Most replies were catcalls from mangy prisoners. Hour after hour, day after day, week after week the girls had continued their vigil until their mouths were raw and their feet sore. Summer waned into autumn, and stiffening north winds brought falling temperatures.

"I wonder if he's aboard one of those prison ships," Rachel said, eyeing the rotted hulks in the harbor. As she spoke, a weighted canvas sack plunged from the nearest ship's quarterdeck and splashed into the water. The dead prisoner sank under a stream of bubbles. Three more sacks followed after him.

"What would you have us do," Sarah said, "row out and surround those wrecks with whistling as well? 'Twill be the surest way to get ourselves berthed in one of them. Rachel, we must face facts. Our grandfather is probably killed."

"I'll not believe it until I see his corpse."

"He may be one of those poor wretches thrown from the ship just now. Rachel, if we tarry in Boston much longer —"

"Hush, Sarah, that sentry is watching us again."

"Why shouldn't he? 'Tis the fourth time this week we've circled the place chirping like birds. I say we get on to the next house before he decides to jail us. In a prison we shan't survive three days."

Rachel battled a swelling fear that Sarah was right. Only by bathing often and dining daily with Col. Dowd had the girls escaped the diseases killing everyone else. Soldiers' corpses were trundled past them by the dozens each day. Every street had houses draped in black flags, and church bells tolled the passing of souls from sunup to sundown. Gravediggers seemed endlessly spading the cemetery earth.

"Oh, God," Rachel prayed for the thousandth time, "please keep Grandfather well. Help us find him."

"I don't see how God can help us at all," Sarah said. "We should never have let Grandfather make that raid. I say we should never have come to Boston at all."

"There's no use wishing we hadn't," Rachel said, "and we can't change anything that's befallen us since. Thus far God has been kind enough to preserve us."

" 'Tis our own good fortune that has kept us unhurt, and who knows how long that may last? Rachel, you must admit to yourself that our grandfather is gone. We are tempting the fates to hunt for him further. I say we leave Boston at once."

"How would you feel, Sarah, if the circumstances were reversed? Suppose you were in prison while Grandfather roamed the streets looking for you. Would you not want him to turn every stone again and again until he had found you?"

"What's the use of speculating so? He's the one jailed, not us."

"All of us are jailed," Rachel said.

"There you go, babbling again. How can you say that when we may roam the streets as we please and can even escape to Cambridge if we choose?"

"Must you take everything so literally? I am speaking of our souls, Sarah."

" 'Tis hard to contemplate the soul when the belly is growling."

"Shortsighted, that's what you are. Try to forget your next meal for a moment and consider that our real troubles are not food and freedom. 'Tis our spirits needing rescue more than anything else. Don't you see that God searches this evil mire for us, to lift us from it? I don't want to give up on Grandfather any more than I want God to give up on me."

"If God is so good, why does He allow this wickedness? I think Him a terrible ogre to permit such misery."

"The world's horrors are man's doing, not God's."

"Rachel, you're impossible. By your reckoning, all of life's woes are our fault."

"Just so, because we reject God's ways and follow after our own."

"Why is that bad? His ways are tedious and dull."

"And ours are selfish and twisted. Really, Sarah, even you must agree we're all stained by greed and malice. If someone has something we want, we take it from him. If we cannot take it, we hate him for it. And if we hate him enough, we may kill him."

"I am hardly so wicked as that. I don't lie or steal. I've never . . . well, I suppose I have killed someone, but he was an evil wretch."

"So you measure goodness by Moses' law. Those are God's rules."

"They're simple common sense, Rachel. Any civilized society would agree to them."

"What of the other commandments? Have you never desired what belonged to someone else?"

"How does one manage that? 'Tis an impossible command to keep."

"Because you're sinful, Sarah. If you were truly upright, as God is, you would have no trouble with it at all."

"But He's God. He needs nothing. Why should He fret Himself about another girl's bonnet or another man's horse?"

"Why should you? Are you so needful of a bonnet that you would injure someone else to have it?"

"I'm sure I don't go about—"

"What of the first commandment, to love the Lord with all your heart and soul and mind and strength?"

"What sort of brute orders himself loved?"

"If we're to be His bride we must love Him," Rachel said. "If we love Him, we will do what pleases Him."

"And if we disagree, He throttles us with calamity and disaster."

"You're missing the point."

"I certainly am."

Rachel frowned.

"Do you hope for a husband?" she said.

"Of course."

"Why?"

"I want children. I want a joyful household."

"To what purpose?"

"I don't know. Why do you ask such silly questions?"

"There's more to having a husband than bearing children by him, Sarah. What do you want most from a husband?"

"I want to be loved."

"Suppose a man is courting you but only because you are the only girl available to him. If he has no choice but to marry you, would you not wonder if he really loved you?"

"I daresay."

"Would it not be delicious, Sarah, to know that your bridegroom ignored every other girl in the county because he desired only you? Imagine seeing him reject girls prettier and wealthier, even girls of noble birth, because he yearned only for you?"

"I should want that very much."

"How much more does God want the same from you? He loves you, Sarah, and He wants you to love Him. Unless you

have a choice in the matter, your affections will be no better than a dog's. So God lets you choose, and He honors the
choice you make."

"What sort of choice is it, to wed good or evil? 'Tis like
choosing between a prince and a drunkard."

"But so many of us choose the drunkard," Rachel said.
"We believe his lies, that he will satisfy and fulfill us. So we
reject God and His goodness, and pursue instead evil and
wickedness. And thus we make drunkards of ourselves. We
become sick with sin and fall so deeply into its pit that we
cannot escape it. We know we should be good, but we cannot bring ourselves to do it. Even when we try, our noblest
efforts are mired in selfish motives. Can you tell me true that
your best deeds are never tainted by secret, selfish desires?"

Sarah bit her lip. Her voice grew soft, and she said, "No."

"Because you are sinful, and so am I. The prophet Isaiah
said that none of us is good, not even one, and our sinful-
ness pollutes everything we do. It is not God who allows the
world's misery. It is we who create it with every selfish action
and every wrong decision we make. But God still loves us,
Sarah. He calls us to leave our darkness and return to His
light. Every one of us must make his choice, to wed ourselves
to God or cleave to our sin."

"And too often we choose badly."

"Look at both of us. You want to give up on searching
for Grandfather. Why? Because it is inconvenient and uncomfortable, perhaps even fatal. I feel the same way. I'm as
discouraged as you and just as tempted to surrender. But
what is the right thing to do? Give up or keep hope alive? Do
we yield to our laziness and fear or continue looking until we
either find him or know certainly that he's dead? God never

gives up on us until we either choose Him or spurn Him. I love Him, and I want to be like Him. So I press on."

"But how do we love God?" Sarah said. "We cannot even see Him."

"He has already shown Himself to us."

"When did He ever do that?"

"He disguised Himself, Sarah. 'Tis just as you and I are doing. We mask ourselves as Regina Silsby and go romping all about Boston, but no one knows that it is really you and I. God has done the same thing. He masked Himself in a man's body and walked through His creation."

"But who . . ."

"Gracious, Sarah, you attend church every Sabbath. Do you not listen to what is said?"

"Most times I am wishing I were somewhere else."

"Jesus of Nazareth is God Almighty clothed in human flesh. His mission was to reconcile us to Himself. 'Tis true God loves us, but His purity cannot tolerate our sin. So He heaped our wickedness on the man Jesus and let Him die with it."

"But if Jesus is really God Himself . . ."

". . . He reclaimed that dead body and raised it to life again. He's still alive, Sarah, and He's still calling to us. 'Tis as though God made it possible for you and me to trade coats with Him. Jesus gives you His righteousness and takes on Himself your wickedness. All you need do is believe that He has done this for you and ask to receive the coat He offers you."

Sarah slowed to a stop.

"Rachel," she said, "I have never done that."

"Then we shall not take another step until you do."

"I don't know how."

" Tis the simplest thing in the world. Speak to Him as you would speak to me, and be confident that He will hear."

"I'm afraid."

"Mercy, Sarah, He's not going to strike you dead."

"But what shall I say?"

"Tell Him you love Him. Say whatever comes to mind."

"Should we not go to a church?"

"Why? He's here with us and has been all along. Now come, sit on this bench with me. Talk to Him as you've heard me do."

Sarah gripped Rachel's hand.

"Dear God," she said, "Rachel tells me that You will hear me. I so want to believe her—I do believe her. I confess that I have been very far from You. My whole life I have lived with no regard for You. Please do not hold it against me. Now I understand how the world's evil is our fault, not Yours. Forgive me for blaming You for it and for failing to see my own hand in it. Please trade coats with me. Take my wickedness from me, and clothe me in Your goodness. Show me how I may make You happy."

She sat silently, sensing nothing. Perhaps He had refused her as she had so often refused Him.

"Don't spurn me, Lord," she said. "I do love You so very much. Help me love You better."

Something stirred within her, like the first hint of a breeze ruffling a sail. The sensation swelled into a rushing wind that swept through her being. She knew at that moment that He *had* heard her, that He was not simply near, but *very* near, and that He had been so all her life, calling to her and waiting for a reply. At last she had recognized His voice and answered. And with her response welled a fresh sensation in her heart. God Himself was dancing for joy—*from inside her.*

A long forgotten catechism returned to her mind.

Whoever opens the door to Me, I will come in and dwell with him, and he with Me . . . and we shall make our home together . . .

The catechism was true. She had opened to Him the portal of her heart, and He had swept through, invading her soul, breathing into her spirit His own life. And with that breath came a strange and wonderful sensation, a certainty that her prayers did not vanish into a void. God Almighty loved her, and from that day forward He would commune with her, fight for her, even die for her. He would never leave her, and now she would never leave Him.

"Dearest Father," she said, gripping Rachel's hand tighter, "please help us. We know not where Grandfather is. But You do. He must be hungry and cold by now. He may be sick, even dying. Take us to him. Show us where they've put him, and if he is gone, please tell us so and make us grateful that he has gone to You. And one other thing I would ask of You. Grant me the same boldness you have given Rachel. Give me a stout heart and a sound mind. Make me more like her. Make me more like You."

She wiped her eyes and shared with her cousin a long gaze. For the first time she recognized the gleam in Rachel's eye. It was the Lord Himself looking back at her through her cousin. And He was smiling.

"Shall we continue with our whistling?" Sarah said.

"There's still time before our noon meal."

"Let us go to back to that stinking hovel by the Lime Street foundry. And then we shall try again at the Charter House."

"Very well."

"Until we find him," Sarah said, "or know for certain he is lost to us."

Arm in arm they strolled the wharves, saying little. Sarah savored the sun's rays on her back and admired the bright shafts penetrating the clouds. Light glittered on the harbor waters, and seagulls spotted the shimmering waves. Other birds crowded the jetties and soared overhead. She drew deep drafts of salt air into her lungs, enjoying its scented chill. A nearby church bell tolled, even as workers stripped away its wooden spire.

At Lime Street the girls approached the foundry's sentinel.

"Good sir," Sarah said to him, "can you tell me how long until the noon hour?"

"Half-past eleven's just tolled," he said.

"Indeed? I did not notice."

She chatted with him while her cousin ambled around the corner. Odors of filth and waste stung her nostrils, and even the guard smelled worse than most, but Sarah jabbered gaily as if nothing foul could ever trouble her again. Rachel returned shaking her head. Sarah promised the guard a return visit, and the girls walked to the Charter House. Hearing no response there, they wandered toward Old North Meeting.

"Col. Dowd will be expecting us at table soon," Rachel said. "I suppose we shouldn't disappoint him."

"What a godsend he has been to us." Sarah said.

"Not that he intends it so."

"He is amusing, is he not? Such ardor resides in that fat breast of his. Were he more agile we should never escape him. But as it is —"

"Look, Sarah, what's that?"

Rachel pointed down a side lane. Soldiers dragged a bound man from an ox cart and hurried him to a house squashed between two larger dwellings. The entry banged shut, and the cart rolled away.

"We haven't been there before," Sarah said. She and Rachel drifted toward the building. Its front wall was mortared round stone with shutters of thick timber barring two windows. There was no sentry, no smoke pluming from the chimney.

Rachel whistled her whippoorwill's cry. After a long silence she tried again.

"Let us check the stable yards behind," Sarah said. "Perhaps no one can hear us from here."

They wandered past the house, searching for a portal or an alley that might lead behind the dwelling. Snarling dogs guarded some passages, bolted gates blocked others. Rachel repeated her whistle while probing corners and testing locks. Sarah hummed along, adding a whistle of two of her own. At last they found an entry that yielded to them. It led to an empty goat pen walled by a planked fence. The girls separated a pair of loose boards and slipped into the neighboring yard. There they climbed a low stone wall to a pigsty. Dry mud crumbled beneath their boots as they approached a high granite wall.

Beyond the barrier clanged a blacksmith's hammer.

"They're forging chains," Sarah said.

Rachel whistled, and the hammering stopped. Her eyes locked with Sarah's, and Sarah shook her head, warning her not to whistle again. Eventually the racket resumed. Sarah pressed her brow to Rachel's and whispered, "I think they know it is a signal."

"Come over by the gate," Rachel said. "I shall try once more, but be ready to run. If we reach the street quickly enough, they will not suspect us."

Sarah nodded. They climbed the stone wall and stood by the fence. Sarah held the planks open while Rachel cupped her hands to her lips.

She whistled again. This time a faint whippoorwill replied—from behind them. Both girls spun around. They scanned the house abutting the fence. Its low roof sagged over a wall of warped clapboards pealing brown paint. Rachel repeated her whistle. A distant cry returned to her. Again the blacksmith's hammering stopped.

"This way," Rachel said, ducking through the fence.

"Careful. It may not be Grandfather."

"Hurry. Someone is climbing the stone wall."

Sarah pressed a hand to her skirt and felt the reassuring presence of her pistol. She bustled with Rachel to the street and plopped onto a bench, pretending to mend a tear in Rachel's hem. No one followed them.

"Are you certain you heard climbing back there?" Sarah said.

"Perhaps they were merely looking over the wall."

Many minutes passed before Rachel felt safe enough to whistle again. The whippoorwill's cry returned more distinctly. They rose and followed the sound along the street. It led them to the corner and down a neighboring lane. At one point the chirping waned, and the girls retraced their steps. When the sound seemed almost above them, they scanned the windows overlooking the street. Rachel whistled again and got an immediate reply.

"Look, Rachel," Sarah said. "In the alleyway—there he is."

Seventeen

❦

Prison

Rachel's heart leapt for joy. In a barred window high above the lane waved a white kerchief. The girls ran to the base of the wall.

"By my faith, children," Grandfather said, peering down at them, "I was beginning to fear I'd never see you again."

"Grandfather," Rachel said, fighting tears, "are you well?"

"Well enough. Food's miserable, water's bad, cell's cold. How do you fare?"

"Sarah and I shall fetch you food and drink straightaway. And we'll find blankets for you as well."

"Bless you, child. I'll not be wandering anywhere."

They scurried down the street.

"Oh, Rachel," Sarah said, "how wonderful. I can hardly believe it."

Rachel crumbled into tears.

"I was so afraid," she said, collapsing in her cousin's arms. "So much death, and so many weeks of nothing. I wondered how he could still be alive."

"It is done now," Sarah said. "God has brought us to him."

"Aye," Rachel said. "Now we must tend him."

At a corner tavern they bought beef, bread, a flagon of stale beer, and a woolen blanket. They carried the meal back to the prison house and hammered on the door. A wrinkled man with black teeth and a missing eye answered, his unshaven face scarred and sweating. Rags covered his stooped shoulders, and a wooden leg thumped the floor. He scowled at the girls.

"I've brought victuals for my father," Rachel said. The jailor squinted at the basket on her arm. He left the door swinging on its hinges and hobbled into the dark chamber beyond. A straw cot and a rough table furnished the room. Rafters and walls were riddled with termite tunnels.

"What's his name?" the jailor said, dropping onto a stool and stretching his bad leg before him. He opened a stained ledger book.

Rachel hesitated. What name had her grandfather supplied his captors? He had used almost a dozen since arriving in Boston.

"I know you have him here," she said. "I saw him in the upper window just now."

"What's his name?"

Despite the man's gnarled hand covering the ledger she managed to scan its scribbled columns.

"Henry Tawney," she said, recognizing one of the names.

The jailor searched the page.

"Very well," he said, and heaved himself from his seat. "What have you brought him?"

"Beef, bread, and ale."

"That's for me, lass. What have you brought him?"

Rachel stood open-mouthed.

"Give it here," he said, reaching for the basket.

"You shall not take this from me."

"Then you shall not see your father."

She stood stiffly, unsure what to do.

If a man requests your shirt, give him your coat as well . . .

"What if I should give it to you?" she said.

"Give it?" he said, puzzled.

"You shall not take it from me, but I will gladly give it to you."

"What's the difference?"

"A point of honor. If I make a gift of this meal to you, may I be assured that you will let me bring another for my father?"

"Fair enough."

"Then please permit me to serve you."

"Suit yourself."

He watched as she spread the food before him.

"Now I shall fetch something for my father," she said. "Come along, sister."

They left him gobbling his meal and tramped back to the tavern.

"That thief," Sarah said, "stealing food from a starving man."

"He's apart from God," Rachel said, "and hardly better off himself. 'Tis just as we discussed."

"Upon my word, you're right. Dear God, bless that man. Let him see how badly he needs You. Show him his errors and . . . good heavens, now I'm doing it."

"What?"

"Praying as you do."

Rachel laughed.

"Let us see how well the poor fellow tolerates our kindness," she said. "We may find ourselves forced upon Grandfather."

They bought a shilling's worth of food and drink and carried it back to the jail.

"There you are," Sarah said while tucking a napkin to the jailor's chin. "Fit for a king, this feast. We brought you more stew and a pease pudding and kidney pie. There's cranberry tarts as well and apple cider to wash it all down."

He blinked his amazement and then attacked his meal.

"What is your name, sir?" Rachel said.

"Foate."

"Is this your dwelling, Mr. Foate, or do you hire it from somebody else?"

" 'Tis my own."

He shoveled the kidney pie between his teeth and guzzled a tankard of cider.

"Sir," Sarah said, "you forgot to bless the meal."

He stared at her, crumbs dropping from his lips.

"Would it not be proper," she said, "to set a pious example by us? After all, you are head of this household. I think it right that you, as master of the house, ask God's blessing on all of us."

"Enough of this," he said. "Come along."

He pulled himself upright, grabbed a key ring from the wall, and clumped to a narrow stair. Rachel and Sarah trailed him to a second floor hallway. There he jammed a key into one of the locked entries.

"Five minutes," he said, pushing open the door. Rachel rushed into Grandfather's arms.

"God bless you, lass," he said. "And here's pretty Sarah too. Such a welcome sight you are."

"We brought a meal," Rachel said, and set her basket on the bare floor.

"You've not been here long," Sarah said, observing the fetid pile of waste in one corner.

"Only a few days," he said. "They've moved me about a time or two. Until I got here I was fed fairly well and able to exercise a bit each day."

He gripped Rachel's shoulder, then pressed a finger to his lips and pointed to the walls. She understood.

"Eat something, Father," she said, and motioned Sarah to start a lively chatter.

"Gracious," Sarah said, responding to her cousin's cue, "you'll not believe the trouble we've had finding you, Father. Col. Smith was a fine help though and finally got us through to Gen. Gage. One of his staff made a great search for us. He was most kind. At any rate, you'll be glad to know that cousin

Randolph is still supplying the officer's mess with meat and meal and . . ."

Rachel pressed her head to Grandfather's.

"How many of you are here?" she said, pretending to fuss over his food.

"Eighteen," he said while ladling stew to his lips. "We lost four in the skirmish and two to disease. I'm locked away from the lads because they think me some sort of ringleader."

"Where are the others?"

"Across the hall. To my left are four redcoat deserters. Sergeants, they were. 'Twill not go well with them. They went over to the rebel camps and were training the militias until they got themselves recaptured. They'll have a noose around their necks for it."

"And you?"

"I shan't fare much better," he said, "after I've lost my use to them."

"What use is that?"

"All sorts of questions they're asking me about the rebel dispositions, the conditions in the camps, the caliber of the officers. They've even asked after Regina Silsby—quite a bit, actually."

"What have you told them?"

"Nary a thing. Tried to make myself look completely daft is what I've done. But there's one major among them who's dangerously clever. He sees through me, I think; otherwise I'd not be alive today."

"You don't seem to be mistreated."

"So far they've left me unhurt. 'Tis the fellows across the hall they're brutalizing and making certain I hear it."

"Do you know the major's name?"

"Can't think of it offhand," he said. "Call . . . Cole . . . something of the sort."

"Cauldon?"

"Aye, that's it. How did you know?"

"I've met him. We must fetch you out of here at once."

"Rachel, dear, don't fret yourself about me. 'Tis a good life I've been blessed to live, and I'll not complain how the Lord chooses to take me from it."

"But what of the others?"

"Don't be foolish, lass. You're talking nearly twenty men."

"Including the deserters?"

"Heavens, child, what do you hope to do, evacuate the entire building?"

"We can't very well fetch you out and leave the others behind. Are you able to communicate with them?"

"A bit."

"Can you tell them something's afoot?"

"Rachel, I won't go to my grave knowing you had died on my account. Give it up, lass. Get you and your cousin back to Philadelphia straightaway."

"I shan't leave without you."

"You mustn't risk another day in Boston."

"My mind's made up, Grandfather. Unless I go with you, I shan't go at all."

"Have you considered your cousin?"

"She's with me, heart and soul."

"There's no talking sense into you, is there?"

"None whatever."

He sighed.

"Then you must take care," he said. "It may not look it, but the redcoats are watching us like hawks."

"How many are there, and where?"

"Not sure, to both questions. Look to the houses on either side and across the street."

"How shall I alert you when we come again? We mustn't whistle. The redcoats know it is a signal."

"No doubt. I've been whistling myself silly since they took me, hoping you might hear. Can you mimic a cat's meow? We'll use that instead. And Rachel, be sure to write a letter to your mother before you try anything. Should you fail, you mustn't leave her wondering whatever became of you."

"Take heart, Grandfather. Sarah and I shall not fail you."

" 'Twould be better if you had never found me at all."

"You would do as much for me, would you not?"

He wrapped his arms around her.

"Go with God, child," he said.

"I love you, Grandfather."

"And I love you, Rachel."

He kissed her brow.

"So, there we stood," Sarah said, "eyeball to eyeball with the most motley rum guzzlers in the colony. The general was most impressive. 'Stand aside, you ruffians,' said he, 'unhand the ladies, or forfeit your lives.' I think he meant it too, for he was already drawing his saber and . . ."

The jailor appeared in the doorway.

"Time's done," he said.

"But I was just getting to the good part of it," she said.

"Off with you, lass. 'Tis a wonder you haven't talked him to death."

"Come, sister," Rachel said, "your story must wait until our next visit."

"Oh, bother," Sarah said. "Very well, if you insist. Good bye, Father. We shall come back with another meal. 'Twill be so much easier, now that we know where to find you."

"Fare well, my daughters," he said. "Don't you fret yourselves on my account. And be sure to thank the good general for me."

The jailor banged shut the door and fastened the lock.

"By the queen's petticoats," he said, thumping down the stairs, "you've enough wind in you to roll a whaler on its beam."

"We're just giddy with seeing him," Sarah said. "In our place you would do the same."

"You've spoken more words in five minutes than I've said in my whole life. Now be gone, the both of you."

He shooed them through the front entry and slammed the door.

"Well, I never," Sarah said, planting her hands on her hips. "How rude. He seems quite incapable of any filial affection at all."

"Come along, sister," Rachel said. "The colonel will worry about us."

Arm-in-arm they bustled down the street.

"What did you learn?" Sarah said. Rachel told her everything.

"Well, this certainly is a pickle," Sarah said. "Eighteen men, plus Grandfather and the deserters? How shall we manage it?"

"First, we will scout the area and mark the placement of the soldiers."

"And then?"

"We must think of way to confound them."

"How exciting."

No sooner had the girls departed than the jailor emerged from his house, crossed the street, and rapped a door opposite.

"Well, what is it?" said the soldier who answered. He stifled a yawn and strapped on his suspenders.

"The major wished to know of any visitors to the Tawney prisoner," said the jailor.

"Has he had any?"

"Just now. Two young women claimed to be his daughters."

"You oaf. Wake me when he has a real visitor."

"The major said *all visitors*. Seems to me that's women as well as men."

"And I say it isn't. Faith, man, you'll have me chasing after every horse and hound that sniffs about your stinking shack. 'Tis rebel traitors and Sons of Liberty we're looking for, not silly women."

"The major wants all visitors reported and tracked," the jailor said. "If you know what's good for you —"

"Be gone, imbecile. Don't show your face here again until a man comes along."

"What's the fuss, private?" said a corporal at his back.

"This old fool says a pair of girls has visited the Tawney prisoner. He wants us to report it to the major and go chasing after them."

"Let's get on it, then," said the corporal, shrugging on his tunic.

"But sir . . ."

" 'Tis America we're in, private, not England. You find a very different sort of woman here. She looks you in the eye and speaks her mind and has as much say in choosing a husband as her father. You, jailor, which way did they go?"

"Down the lane toward Dock Square."

"Private, you report to the major. I'll catch up to them."

Eighteen

A Scolding

"Idiot," Maj. Cauldon said. He slapped the corporal with his riding crop. "How could you let them escape you?"

"I'm most sorry, sir. The streets were crowded, and . . ."

"Did you see them at all?"

"They had a long start on me, sir, but I followed after them as best I could. At Dock Square I lost them, but they must have gone on to Cornhill or King Street."

"Why do you think I've posted so many men about that jail? We can't expect old Foate to be our only eyes and ears. Had you been more vigilant, we'd have them in irons by now."

"He said they were two young women, sir. Quite pretty."

"What else did he say?"

"One was dark-haired, the other fair. Average height, healthy complexions . . ."

"You imbecile. Such a description could match any of these Boston wenches."

"They'll be returning, sir. They promised to bring the prisoner another meal."

"That Tawney fellow knows much more than he's letting on. What the devil is he hiding?"

"Begging your pardon, sir, but the lads are convinced he's out of his mind. You yourself have seen how he babbles and slobbers."

"He's played you all for fools, Corporal. I shouldn't be at all surprised if he's in league with Regina Silsby. Were he younger I'd suspect him of being the ghost himself."

"There's talk among the men, sir, of a pretty pair of girls who've been seen all about town. I wonder if . . ."

"What?"

"It seems they're everywhere, sir, strolling here, sitting there. Sisters, they are. Many of the lads have talked to them, but no one seems to know where they come from. I wonder if they could be the same persons who visited the prisoner."

"Sisters, you say? Making their home near Dock Square? One dark, the other fair?"

"Sounds like a nursery rhyme, sir."

"Hold your tongue."

"I'm sorry, sir."

Cauldon paced the room, hammering a fist to his chin. Why did that seem familiar? He had first seen Regina Silsby near Dock Square, on the night he had escorted Miss Jennifer and Miss Sarah home.

"Strike me dead," he said, halting. "But that can't be. No, it is impossible, surely. Unless . . ."

"Sir?"

"Never mind. Post guards at Dock Square. See to them yourself, Corporal. Keep watch for these two young women. Report to me the moment you know their lodgings. We'll double the guard at the prison house as well. No, triple it. If these girls show their faces again, you're to follow them home yourself. I want them found, Corporal, understood? Fail again, and I'll see every man in your company horsewhipped."

"Aye, sir."

"There's another soldier," Sarah said. "That's fifteen we've counted."

"Let me see."

Rachel accepted the spyglass and peered through the lattice of the Christ Church belfry. So high above the rooftops were they that people wandering the streets seemed mere ants. Birds soared over distant chimneys, some of them climbing as high as the bell tower and perching on the sills at the girls' feet. A boarded scaffold wrapped the steeple chasm at their backs, and in the peaked grotto hung the church's great bronze bell.

"The window of that dwelling behind the prison," Sarah said. "You can see him looking into the alley."

"We've not observed anyone in that house before. That makes three dwellings they've put to use as guard posts."

"Heaven knows why so many soldiers are needed to secure a jail. All this trouble for a lot of condemned men."

"I'll wager they're working in three watches," Rachel said, "eight men per watch, for a total of twenty-four."

"With a sergeant over each and perhaps an officer. Rachel, that could mean as many as thirty."

"We've seen them march out for drilling in groups of eight with a sergeant and an officer going along."

"Could they have posted one watch to guard the house while another sleeps and the third exercises?" Sarah said.

"That sounds reasonable."

"Meaning only eight men at a time are posted around the place."

"But those sleeping can be mustered at a moment's notice," Rachel said. "And they must have a signal for summoning the ones drilling."

"If we move quickly, we may fetch Grandfather away before they return. Then we would face no more than sixteen."

"How very comforting."

"Perhaps we could arm Grandfather and his fellows."

"Where will we get the weapons? Besides, his men are tortured and starved and in no condition to fight. No, we must draw off the redcoats somehow."

"I don't see a way," Sarah said. "Do you recall that ruckus two nights ago when the rebels floated those batteries into the Charles River? Every soldier in Boston ran out to fire upon them except these fellows. 'Twas the same last night with that cannonade from the ferry ways."

" 'Tis as though they were waiting for something," Rachel said. "If Grandfather were here, he'd smell a trap."

"Who would they be hoping to catch?"

"Regina Silsby, perhaps. Grandfather said they were asking after her."

"We shan't easily frighten a pack of soldiers expecting a surprise," Sarah said. "Are you certain we heard God aright about this?"

"We spent three days fasting and praying through it," Rachel said, "and we both sensed His permission to proceed."

"I don't see how we can manage without getting killed. A memorable rescue that would be."

"If we waited for a fog or a rainfall . . ."

" 'Twould slow us as well as them."

"But foul weather would make their muskets unusable."

"And if they decide to march Grandfather off to a gallows before a rain comes? I say we move quickly, Rachel. We haven't been back to see him since our first visit."

"It hasn't seemed safe. You said as much yourself."

"He must be wondering after us by now. Why do you keep staring at that water mill?"

"It may prove useful. I wonder . . ."

Sarah sat on the wooden walk with her feet dangling over the precipice. From a satchel she slipped a loaf of bread.

"How I wish we were back in Philadelphia," she said, tearing off a chunk and handing it to Rachel. "There we'd have nothing to vex us but the upcoming masques."

"The what?"

"Have you never been to one? They're all the rage this time of year. Everyone dresses in outlandish costumes for the masked balls on All Hallow's Eve. There's dancing and feasting, games of all sorts. We spend the evening trying to guess who's behind each mask. At midnight all the masks come off, so everyone can see how well they guessed."

"That doesn't sound too difficult."

"It is not, really, but it is great fun. I like so much disguising myself. I've gone as a bird and a cat. Once I went as the Delphi Oracle, and another year I dressed myself as . . ."

Her voice trailed off. Rachel was staring at her.

"Is something wrong?" Sarah said.

"You've given me a splendid idea. We'll have a masked ball of our own, and those extra soldiers shall be a godsend to us."

Nineteen

❧

The Masque

A single candle brightened the girls' bedchamber. In the wardrobe hung their cloaks and masks, along with loaded pistols, a pair of kitchen knives, and other sundries they had gathered for their escapade. Rachel's map was spread on the bed.

"The guards are posted here, here, and here," she said, indicating the spots. "This house's watch will be sleeping tonight, and these eight will be exercising behind Beacon Hill."

"When is the low tide?" Sarah said.

"Three hours hence. You understand our tricks and traps?"

"Of course. Do you take me for a simpleton? What is keeping Col. Dowd? Usually he's knocked on our door by this time."

"Maddening, is it not? The one night we wish him to call upon us, he refrains."

Hardly had Rachel finished speaking when a thump jiggled the door.

"Miss Sarah, Miss Rachel, are you within?" the colonel said.

"Upon my word," Rachel said, pocketing the map. "Could that be Col. Dowd? Sarah, do see who's in the hall."

"Good evening, ladies," the colonel said when Sarah pulled open the door. "I do hope you haven't had your supper yet. I've quite a feast ordered for us downstairs."

"Colonel, you're too endearing," Sarah said. "We're simply famished."

"We'll make a merry night of it," he said. "Miss Rachel, I'd be so grateful if you'd start us with a jolly tune on the clavichord."

"My pleasure, Colonel. I'm glad my playing pleases you."

" 'Tis rare that one so talented can also be so beautiful."

"You flatter me," she said, accepting the arm he offered her. "I must say you look splendid in your uniform."

"I had it laundered today, just for you."

They descended to the parlor.

"Innkeeper," Dowd said. "We'll have a bottle of your best sherry. Be quick about it, man."

Rachel seated herself at the clavichord and played a lively melody. Dowd filled and refilled the glasses, singing all the while and never noticing that the girls used their refreshments to water the plants. He laughed with them over a game of backgammon and feasted merrily in the dining room before returning to the parlor for more games and singing.

"My sacred stars," he said with a yawn. "Is it already nine o'clock?"

"Oh, you cannot be tired just yet," Sarah said. "Rachel, play that jig again. Colonel, be a dear and dance it for us once more."

He demonstrated jigs and hornpipes until he was too weary to remain upright. With the innkeeper's help the girls hauled him to his chamber.

"Be sure to hang up the colonel's uniform," Rachel said. "He's just had it laundered and will certainly raise a ruckus if it's soiled."

"Aye, Miss."

"You'll tally everything to the colonel's tariff, of course."

"Already done," said the innkeeper while peeling off Dowd's tunic. "I'll see that he's properly put to bed. Good night, missies."

The girls retreated to their own room, closed the door, and pressed their ears to the panel. Dowd's singing echoed in the hall while the innkeeper stripped him to his skivvies and tucked him between the sheets. Loud snores filled the room before the door closed, and the innkeeper's footsteps tramped down the stairs.

Back across the hall the girls crept, and into the colonel's chamber.

"On the chair by the window," Rachel said. "His tunic, breeches, and stockings are all there."

"What about his hat?"

"Check the wardrobe. And don't forget his sword."

"I have it already and his boots."

They returned to the hall and locked Dowd's door from the outside.

"I feel myself a thief," Sarah said, dropping the key into a spittoon filled with sludge.

"We'll send it back when we're done with it," Rachel said. "Let's be off."

They folded the colonel's uniform into a sack, gathered their belongings, and descended the stair. While the innkeeper busied himself in the larder, they slipped through the back entry to a neighboring alley. There they donned their ghosts' masks, whispered a final prayer together, and paced the dark streets. First they visited a storehouse used by the British quartermaster and then a fishery near the ferry ways. At the water mill they waited until Cauldon had marched his eight men toward Beacon Hill. Steeple towers chimed ten o'clock.

"Perfect," Rachel said. "On to the next chore."

After running cables and stringing tackle blocks, they approached Grandfather's prison.

"Yonder is the first sentry," Rachel said, "just as we expected. Are you ready?"

Sarah nodded. She arranged her hood a final time, stepped from the shadows, and drifted down the lane.

"Hold," said the guard as she brushed past him. "I say, woman, what's your business here?"

She turned her face to him. He recoiled, aghast. From behind Rachel clubbed him with her pistol. He crumpled to the pavement, and the girls dragged him behind a picket gate. They stripped off his uniform, and Rachel carried it away. Sarah rolled the fallen man behind a rain barrel.

"You there," said a gruff voice, "what are you about?"

A musketed soldier stood over her.

"Goodness, sir, how you frightened me," she said, hiding her face in the folds of her cloak. "This poor fellow—I found him in the gutter here. Someone has robbed him, I think."

The soldier stooped over the stricken man.

"By my faith," he said. " 'Tis Rawlins, probably drunk again. Heavens, why is he undressed?"

Rachel's pistol rapped the soldier's skull. A minute later he lay half-naked with his comrade. Both men were bound wrist and ankle, and their mouths knotted with rags.

"At this rate we'll have everything we need in short order," Sarah said. "Another two guards are patrolling the far side of the building."

"The sack's already full. We'll need something larger to store the uniforms."

"Look yonder, Rachel. That ox cart will do nicely."

Beyond the crossroads stood a small wagon. Harnessed to the rig was a horse munching fodder. Two soldiers hefted a keg into the wagon bed.

"Careful with that, you louts," said a sergeant. He disappeared with the pair into a stable, leaving one soldier to guard the cart.

"How long have they been there?" Rachel said.

"Why fret about it? 'Tis just what we need, Rachel. Come along."

They slipped to the far side of the wagon and bludgeoned the sentry. His companions struggled through the stable entry with another keg, and the girls struck them down as well. The sergeant cursed his men for dropping the cask until he himself was hammered in the doorway. All four men were dragged into the barn, stripped of their uniforms, and tied hand and foot.

"That makes six," Sarah said while piling the trophies into the cart, "plus the colonel's."

"What's in these kegs, I wonder?" Rachel said. With her pistol butt she knocked a wooden plug from one. Black sand spilled from the cask. Sarah pressed a pinch to her tongue.

"Gunpowder," she said.

"Seven barrels. Gen. Washington could certainly put these to good use."

"So may we. Rachel, this is perfect. You said we needed one more distraction to draw the garrison away from the town gate. Here it is. Let's set a charge somewhere and touch it off as we flee."

"The North Battery. All Boston shall go running there while we head south."

Quickly they modified their plans to accommodate the explosives. A short trip to the North Battery had their diversion set, and on the way back they confiscated two more uniforms. One by one they snared and bound the sentries still pacing the prison, and finally they burglarized the eight men sleeping through their off-watch. Before leaving the barracks they passed a rope through a window, along the floor, and out the entry.

"Nineteen uniforms," Sarah said as Rachel lashed the line to an empty wagon, "with muskets and cartridge pouches, plus twelve bayonets. 'Tis better than we bargained for."

"Let's get the uniforms up to Grandfather," Rachel said. "And keep those guns from rattling against each other like that. One spark will blow us into heaven."

"How many uniforms can you fit in the sack?"

"Only two or three. We'll have to make several runs."

"Why not fish the rope through the sleeves and leggings, and knot the end of it so they won't fall off? I can stuff the stockings in pockets, and we'll put the boots in the sack."

"Get started on it," Rachel said. "I'll alert Grandfather."

She slipped into the alley and mimicked a cat's meow. Carriages rumbled over the nearby cobbles. Footsteps came and went. A cat slunk by, and rats climbed the rubbish heaps. Rachel mewed louder and louder, thinking herself the most obnoxious feline in the city. From the mouth of the alley Sarah watched, her chore done.

At last Grandfather appeared at his window.

"I'm passing something up to you," Rachel said.

"What is it?" he said.

"Uniforms."

"How's that?"

She retreated to the ox cart, and with Sarah she lugged the roped garments into the alley.

"They're so heavy," Sarah said. "He'll never get them up there in one haul."

Rachel tied a rock to the rope's end, and after several throws her grandfather snagged it.

"Mercy, Rachel," he said while pulling the bundle up the wall, "how many have you got here?"

"One for each of you."

He heaved them to the barred window.

"It won't go through," he said. "I'll have to unstring them one by one."

"Rachel, someone's coming," Sarah said. The girls melted into the shadows. A guard wandered past the alley, noticed the ox cart, and started toward it. Rachel darted from her hiding place.

"Excuse me, sir," she said. "I am new to Boston. Can you help me? I must find the Province house."

He turned to answer and glimpsed her face. A scream formed in his throat. She clubbed him unconscious and rolled him into the gutter. In the alley Grandfather struggled with the bundled uniforms. The garments slipped from his grip and plummeted to the pavement.

"Drat," he said. "Rachel, the thing's too heavy. You'll have to strip them off and send them two or three at a time."

"Lord, have mercy," she said. Sarah helped her unstring all but three uniforms. Again Rachel bound a rock to the rope and hurled it to Grandfather. He tied the cord to a window bar and dragged up the lightened load. After dumping the uniforms into his chamber, he let fall the rope's loose end. The girls strung more garments, and Grandfather lifted them to his room. Eventually he had all of them.

"Well done, lasses," he said. "What's next?"

"We must unlock your cell," Rachel said. "Listen for us in the hallway."

The girls approached the prison entry and rapped its bolted door.

"Open," Rachel said in her toad's voice. "Foate, you old horse, do you hear? Open, I say."

She hammered a second time, jiggled the latch, and knocked again. Sarah watched the road and the nearby windows.

"What's keeping you, old man?" Rachel said. "Come along, where are you?"

The door swung wide.

"What the devil do you mean, barging in at this hour?" said a soldier blocking the entry. Rachel struck him numb and bounded over his collapsing form. Sarah sprang after her and bolted shut the door. They listened for a commotion in the street.

"All's quiet," Sarah said. "So far so good. Where's the jailor?"

"Check the cot."

"It is empty."

Rachel probed the wall behind the table.

"I can't find the key ring," she said. "It is not on the peg."

"Rachel, I don't like this."

"Get that fellow's musket. If we must we'll break in the doors."

"Suppose more soldiers are in the house. And where's old Foate?"

"Let's look about."

They searched the downstairs rooms. All were vacant or bolted shut, and no sounds emanated from the locked chambers.

"Give me the musket," Rachel said, "and have your pistol ready. We may get a nasty surprise upstairs."

Slowly they climbed the stairway, Rachel in front clutching the musket, Sarah behind gripping her pistol. The ascent was black and narrow, and the boards creaked with every step. At the top stair Rachel peeked around the corner wall.

Moonlight streamed through a window at the far end of the corridor.

"What do you see?" Sarah said.

"Nothing. Perhaps old Foate went out and took his keys with him."

"Let us get on with it then before he comes back."

Rachel padded down the hall and softly knocked on Grandfather's door.

"Henry Tawney," she whispered through the keyhole. "Can you hear me?"

"Aye, lass."

"Stand back. We haven't got a key."

She raised the musket over the door lock.

"Try to do it in one thrust," Sarah said. "Too much hammering will bring everyone around."

Rachel battered the brass with the gun butt. A loud crack echoed along the hallway. The girls stood paralyzed, listening. Rachel hammered the lock a second time, and a third. At last the door shuddered open.

"Well done, lass," Grandfather said. "Where are the guards?"

"Gone," Rachel said, "or lying in the gutters."

"What's the plan?"

"Dress your men in these uniforms. You're to chase Regina Silsby through Boston Gate and over the Neck. The soldiers will think you're comrades."

"Ought to work."

She shoved a sketched map into his palm.

"You must follow this route exactly," she said. "Sarah and I have arranged some distractions for the soldiers. You're to join up with us at the last crossroads before Boston Gate."

"Give me that musket, and let's get to moving."

"We'll wait for you on the stair."

"Watch your backside. I'll be making a bit of noise."

"Hurry on, then."

Two blows had one door flying open.

"Hush, lads," Grandfather said into the cell. "Up with you, quick now. We're cutting cables."

He hammered a second door open, and a third. The hall was soon crowded with murmuring men. A fourth door yielded the British deserters.

"There's redcoat uniforms in my chamber there," Grandfather said. "Each of you get yourselves dressed in one."

"Glory be," someone said. "Where did these come from? Look, lads—a colonel's tunic. Ho, Captain, you're in charge of this expedition. I say you're the one to wear it."

"Saints alive," Grandfather said. "I could fit three men my size into this jacket. Hurry and get you dressed. We'll be chasing Regina Silsby through the town gate."

"Regina Silsby? You can't mean the ghost."

"She's at the stairwell."

"Faith, man, you're not serious."

Rachel emerged from the shadows.

"On my mother's grave," someone said. "She's real as the rest of us."

"And she's ordered us to fetch her across Boston Neck," Grandfather said.

"Through the embankments? We'll be killed."

"Not while she's protecting us. Come on, mates, who's ready?"

"Sir, how can we be sure . . ."

"Hear me well, lad. Stay in your cell, and you'll hang for certain. Follow Regina Silsby, and take the chance to have your life back."

"Captain, sir, we've a problem. James and Adam are fairly beaten. They can't even stand up."

"Carry them," Rachel said in her frog's voice. All heads turned toward her.

"You heard her, lads," Grandfather said, "let's get onto it, quick now. Not another word until I say."

Rachel vanished around the corner and urged Sarah down the stair. At the bottom step a dark shape crossed their path. Rachel gasped and swung her pistol, battering the intruder to the floor.

"Who was that?" Sarah said.

"Another soldier, I think."

" 'Tis old Foate, Rachel. He must have come from the back."

"Is there anyone else?"

They listened. Rachel gripped Sarah's shoulder and said, "I'll finish up here. Get you to the water mill."

"Done."

Uniformed prisoners padded down the stairs. Rachel pointed a bony hand to the back chamber.

"Look here, lads," Grandfather said. "Sailcloth. Come on, then."

He passed canvas sheets to his comrades. In the front room they rigged stretchers across the stoutest men's shoulders and bundled the wounded into them. Rachel cracked open the entry, surveyed the street, and nodded to Grandfather.

"Righto, lads," he said. "Everyone ready for a run?"

"Hear, hear. Push on."

"Very well, here goes." He drew a deep breath and shouted, "There she be, lads, after her."

Rachel flung open the door and leapt into the street, trampling a soldier. The uniformed prisoners stampeded after her, two pairs of them carrying canvas hammocks. Grandfather grabbed the startled sentry.

"Where did she run off to?" he said.

"Who, sir?" said the guard.

"Regina Silsby, you blind fool. She tried to free the prisoners."

"Yonder," said one of Grandfather's crimson troops.

"After her," Grandfather said.

"Hold," said the sentry. "Beg pardon, Colonel, sir, but where are you taking those injured men?"

"Bewitched them, she has," Grandfather said. "One moment they were standing guard as soberly as you, and the next they were flat on their backs babbling like lunatics. We're off to the apothecary with them. Run and tell the major."

Rachel rushed to the water mill.

"Turn out," shouted the soldier. "Regina Silsby has tried to free the prisoners."

An iron triangle clattered. Candlelight brightened the barracks' window.

"Now, Sarah," Rachel said. "Open the flume."

Sarah swung an ax across the anchor line. A counterweight dropped, and the trough's wooden gate lifted. Torrents cascaded through the sluice and splashed against the giant water wheel. Timbers groaned. Slowly the wheel stirred, hesitated, and turned on its axis. Paddles churned the current to a roiling froth. A rope wrapping the axle tightened. Across the lane and into the barracks stretched the cable, writhing and humming. Men shrieked.

"Regina Silsby's bewitched us."

"Turn out, you cowards, double-time."

"Sir, my uniform's gone."

The empty wagon sprang to life. Up the barracks' step it bumped and banged, and jammed itself against the entry. Doorposts snapped. The wagon crashed through the wall and collapsed in a shower of shattered beams.

"That should busy them for a bit," Rachel said.

"Jolly good," Sarah said, "I'm off to my next station."

"Watch for my signal from the hill yonder. After you've struck your blow, hurry on to the battery. I'll await you at North Square."

Sarah scampered off, and Rachel boarded the ox cart.

"Move along, beast," she said, flicking the reins. The cart rumbled up the slope to the quartermaster's storehouse. At a crossroads crowning the rise, she dismounted. Two lanterns waited beneath a nearby step, and she carried them into the roadway. Farther down the hill stood the miller, scratching his head and examining his spinning water wheel. Soldiers sprinted toward the barracks.

"Clear away this wreckage," yelled an officer. "Captain Styles, what happened?"

"Regina Silsby made an attempt on the prisoners. Hurry and get us out of here. She mustn't escape."

"You heard the captain, men. Remove this rubble."

"Sir, look atop the hill yonder."

"By my faith, there she stands. Fix bayonets and charge the hill."

"But sir, she's . . . she's glowing."

"Imbecile! She holds two lamps in her hands."

Rachel raised high her lanterns and fixed her gaze on the troops stampeding toward her. As they neared the wine-maker's warehouse, she dropped her arms. Steel thumped on wood. Something crashed in the winery, and a whirring of whips thrashed the air. Ropes lining the gutters went taut. A trawler's net sprang from the pavement, snaring a handful of soldiers and hauling them skyward. They dangled screaming from a hoist above the warehouse entry.

"You men, cut them down," said the officer. "The rest of you, follow after me."

Thunder rumbled in the winery. The pavement trembled. Through the warehouse's double doors burst an avalanche of giant casks. One shattered, spilling torrents of wine. Its carcass was crushed beneath the barrels rolling behind. Men screamed and scattered.

"Rally, you fools," bellowed the officer.

Rachel detected a drumming of boots at her back. Troops jogged toward her from Beacon Hill.

"Maj. Cauldon," she said. "How very prompt."

"Sir," said a man at the major's side, "there she is atop the rise."

"Regina Silsby," Cauldon said, drawing his sword. "On my oath, she's a devil's deuce. Forward, men. I want her alive."

His soldiers stormed the hill, slipping and stumbling on the cobbles. Six casks of whale oil the girls had rolled from the quartermaster's stores were spilled over the street until the entire lane was slick with fuel. Rachel dashed a lantern to the moist stones. Fire flared in the roadway and streaked toward the troops. They dove squealing into alcoves and troughs. Her remaining lamp she left in the crossroads and mounted the cart. A whack sent the horse lumbering from the blaze.

"Maj. Cauldon, she's gone."

"Impossible."

At the next crossroads she turned aside. Flames atop the hill faded, and boots pounded the slope. She steered through twisted alleys toward North Square. The clamor trailing her drew nearer.

"Faster, you lazy nag," she said, prodding the horse and peering over her shoulder. A thunderclap shook the ground. Windows shattered. For several moments the lane was bright as day. Above the North Battery a fireball rolled into the sky.

"She's blown the battery," Cauldon said. "This way, you mongrels."

Windows facing the street brightened. Sashes banged open, and heads popped out.

"Fire at the battery," men shouted. Civilians and soldiers tumbled from doorways and rushed toward the ferry ways.

Bells pealed alarm. Rachel ignored the bustle. At North Square she halted and sat hunched beneath her cape.

"My uniform," yelled a half-naked man running among the crowd. "She's taken my uniform."

Someone shoved a pail into his hand and told him to hurry on to the battery. The square soon emptied. From the waterfront bounded a billowing cloak with a milky hand clutching the hood's clasp.

"Grand, was it not?" Sarah said while climbing to Rachel's side. "My ears are still ringing."

The cart jolted forward.

"Keep your face hidden," Rachel said as fresh mobs poured past them. "We mustn't be seen until we're at the gate."

"This is simply splendid," Sarah said. "In such bedlam no one shall think to bother us."

" 'Tis better than we hoped for."

Near the town gate the panic finally subsided. Sarah reloaded her pistol, and Rachel steered into a byway.

"Grandfather should be waiting with the others in the next lane," she said.

"Aye, there they are."

Two dozen men in red tunics crowded the alley. Their excited whispers quieted as the cart rolled toward them.

"You men, listen well," Rachel said in her toad's voice. "We're bound for Boston Neck. Your hardest run is yet ahead of you."

"Regina Silsby," Grandfather said, "may we lay these two invalids in the wagon? The sentries will stop us for certain if we're carrying them."

"They'll be bedded with a cartload of gunpowder," she said. "You there, come forward. Aye, you. Pass a musket to each man. You'll look more like proper soldiers."

Timidly the man dispersed the weapons and cartridge pouches. Grandfather leaned to Rachel's side.

"Lass," he said into her ear, "how do you expect to see us through?"

"We shall make a mad dash along the roadway," she said, "while you chase after us. The redcoats won't shoot at you, since you're dressed as they are. A mile more and we shall be at the rebel lines."

"Suppose the ramparts are gated shut."

She stared at him.

"Didn't quite think of everything, did you?" he said.

A cannon boomed. The shot screamed overhead and splattered into the mud flats.

"Cambridge," Grandfather said as he climbed aboard the wagon. "The rebels are stirring up a ruckus. Probably spied that blast at the North Battery and decided to mount some antics of their own."

He searched among the kegs crowding the wagon bed.

"Ah, here we are," he said, holding aloft a coil of twine. "The good Lord does indeed provide. Quick fuse, by the feel of it. Have you a knife, Regina Silsby?"

She passed a blade to him, and he cut a six-foot length of cord.

"About ten seconds' worth," he said, and shoved one end into a smaller cask's pour hole. With the wooden plug he fixed the cord in place.

"This should open a locked gate," he said. "Let's have your pistol, Regina Silsby. I'll use the firelock to light the fuse."

More cannons thundered. A nearby chimney disintegrated. The British embankments awakened with drums and shouts. Field guns soon barked in reply.

"Come on, lads," Grandfather said above the din. "We'll use the distraction to advantage. Get those wounded men aboard the wagon here."

The invalids were cradled in the cart and covered with canvas.

"If the gate's closed," Grandfather said, "we'll run the wagon up against it and drop off our little bomb here. Once it blows, we'll charge straight through the rubble. Mr. Hardy, you're in charge of the footmen. Everyone make sure his musket's loaded and primed. If you've got a bayonet, get it mounted."

Steel clattered as the men fastened pikes to muzzles. Grandfather surveyed his troops and seemed satisfied.

"Shall we drive on, Regina Silsby?" he said. "If the Lord is kind, we'll break through on the first pass. Hardy, follow after us."

"Righto, sir."

Rachel snapped the reins. The wagon jerked forward, flinging Grandfather down on the injured men.

"Sorry, mates," he said, picking himself up. "Not as steady as I used to be."

"We'll make it through right enough," they said. "Don't you fret about us, sir."

"Boston Gate's dead ahead," Rachel said, "and the ramparts are just beyond. Make ready."

"Hold," called the sentry at the bricked arch. The wagon careened past him and bounced through the open tunnel.

"Idiot," Hardy shouted as his troops sprinted behind. "Why didn't you stop her? That was Regina Silsby."

"Sir, I . . ."

"What's your name?"

"Gordon, sir, forty-seventh."

"Tomorrow morning I shall report you for letting unauthorized persons pass this gate. Now stand aside. Move along, you sorry togs, after her. And you, Gordon, don't let this happen again."

"No, sir. Of course not, sir."

The men raced through the arch and down the Neck. Gun emplacements flashed, and shells streaked across the sky.

"The rampart gate's closed," Grandfather said. "Straight up to it, lass. I've an idea I'd like to try first. If it doesn't work, turn your back to the gate and be ready to fly."

He stood gripping the driver's bench, the tails of his scarlet uniform flapping in the wind. Soldiers on the parapets ignored him.

"Open the gate," Grandfather shouted at the sentries, "Gen. Gage's orders."

"You'll have to show your papers, sir."

"Dash the papers. Get this gate open. There's a bomb just outside about to blow up the earthworks."

The guards exchanged glances.

"What's going on here?" said a lieutenant. "Colonel, sir, may I inquire —"

"Blast you, man," Grandfather said, "we've just got word of a rebel plot to blow up the earthworks. The cannonade is a diversion. Let me out there so I can disarm it."

The lieutenant eyed the cloaked figures huddled on the driver's bench. He reached up and pulled away Rachel's hood. She snarled at him. Grandfather leapt the rail and battered him senseless.

"Throw down the keg," he said. Sarah dove behind the driver's bench and rolled the fused cask off the back. It smacked the cobblestones and wobbled toward the timber gate. Soldiers ran. Grandfather held the pistol's firelock to the cord. The gun flashed and the fuse sparked to life.

"Get you going," he shouted. Rachel whipped the horse away from the gate. Grandfather sprinted after her.

"They're exploding the entry," yelled a guard while dragging his wounded comrade from the wall. A sergeant ran to the keg and yanked loose the fuse. It sputtered out.

"Thunderation," Grandfather said. "Sarah, let's have your pistol."

She pitched it to him. He clicked back the hammer and drew a bead on the cask. The sergeant scrambled away. Grandfather fired and the keg erupted, blowing out the timbered barrier and hurling its shattered carcass across the landscape. Soldiers tumbled to the ground.

"Go," Grandfather said. He hoisted himself into the wagon bed as Rachel flogged the horse. The cart bounded through the flaming hole.

"She's done it," shouted a uniformed prisoner. "Come on, lads, let's get after her."

The crimson mob charged the opening. Muskets banged atop the earthworks, and bullets spattered dirt at the fleeing men's feet. Cannon fire glittered on the distant riverbank. Shots gouged holes in the British embankments and spewed geysers in the river.

"Hold up beyond that bluff yonder, lass," Grandfather said. "We'll be out of musket range there."

The cart rumbled over a ridge. Rachel reined the panting horse beneath a clump of trees.

"By my faith, children," Grandfather said, "that was well done, very well done indeed. You men in the back there, how fare you? The ride wasn't too bumpy, was it?"

"All's well in the wagon bed, Captain. Told you we'd pull through all right."

"Goodness, look there," Sarah said. She leaned over the rail and studied the wagon's side. Bullets had rutted the planks and scarred the wheel spokes.

"A bit close, that," Grandfather said. " 'Tis only by the grace of God we weren't blown sky high."

A crimson line trotted over the hill.

"Ho, lads, what say you?" Grandfather said. "We've done it, by jingo. Every man of you is free and clear."

"And better armed as well," they said. "Three cheers for the Captain, and three cheers for Regina Silsby."

They shouted hurrahs.

"Have we lost anyone?" Grandfather said.

"Not a soul, sir."

"Good show. Let's get off these red coats before we're shot in them."

He stripped to his shirtsleeves and tossed his tunic in the road.

"What say we fire them?" someone said.

"Hear, hear."

With a dollop of gunpowder and a spark from a pistol flint, they set the coats aflame.

"The colonel won't be liking that," Sarah said as the bonfire brightened the road.

"Who goes there?" came a shout from the rebel pickets.

"Friends," Grandfather said. "Patriot friends approaching the line."

"Show yourselves."

"Move ahead, Regina Silsby," Grandfather said, "steady as she goes."

Rachel prodded the horse forward. Across a valley and up a low rise the cart rolled, toward a breastworks bristling with sharpened stakes.

"Halt," said the sentry. "State your name."

"Henry Tawney," Grandfather said, "just back from raiding the British shipping."

"You're not the fellows we lost last summer, are you?"

"The very same. We've a wagonload of gunpowder for Col. Tims."

"You'll find him at the Vassal House, and glad he'll be to see it. Pass, friend."

Rachel flicked her reins and the cart bumped down the road. A crowd gathered.

"Look there. 'Tis the harbor raiders," men said. "Mercy, lads, we'd given you up for lost."

One of the prisoners ran to Rachel's side.

"Upon my word, Regina Silsby," he said. "Ugly you may be, but I shall love you to my dying day. God bless you."

"By my faith," someone said. " 'Tis the Boston ghost that's brought them back."

Regina Silsby's name rippled through the throng. Sarah tugged Rachel's sleeve and said, "How shall we pry ourselves from this?"

"I've no idea," Rachel said. "Armies wanting to kill us we can escape, but the admiration of our comrades?"

Cambridge's candlelit windows brightened the lane ahead. Rachel halted the cart.

"We must depart," she said in her toad's voice. "This night my sister and I have done you a service. Now we shall return to our rest."

"Regina Silsby," Grandfather said, "where may we find you if you're needed again?"

She spied a church spire on the horizon.

"There," she said, "among the graves. Come, sister, the dawn approaches."

"You heard her, lads," Grandfather said. "Stand aside and let them pass."

The girls descended to the ground and glided through the parting throng. Men bowed low, tipping their hats.

"Godspeed, Regina Silsby," they said. "Fare you well."

Past the fringes of Cambridge the girls wandered, and into the empty fields beyond.

"May we remove our masks now?" Sarah said.

"I think it is safe."

Sarah peeled off her leather hide and flung wide her arms.

"Goodness, Rachel," she said, spinning around, "what a romp that was. I've never been so terrified or so exhilarated. Wasn't it grand?"

"It is not done yet," Rachel said. "We've yet a little problem to solve."

"Which is?"

"Where shall we go? We can't very well return to Boston."

"Aye, Col. Dowd will want his uniform back."

"Nor can we go to Tims or Washington. If Regina Silsby appears tonight with Grandfather, and we show ourselves tomorrow at the breakfast table . . ."

"I see your point. What shall we do?"

"We'll go to that church yonder and wait for Grandfather to come find us."

"And after that?"

Rachel shrugged.

❧

A buckskinned sentry ran to the step of the Vassal House.

"Col. Tims, sir, Gen. Washington, sir," he said, saluting, "the harbor raiders have returned. Regina Silsby brought them back to us."

"Upon my word," Washington said. "Is that she at the cart there?"

"Aye, sir, and that's her sister beside her. God bless the both of them, I say. They've brought back our missing men, and five kegs of gunpowder besides."

"Fetch her here," Washington said. "I'll have a word with her."

"Sir, she's gone," Tims said, indicating the empty driver's bench. "There she goes through the crowd. Shall I run and bring her to you?"

"Let her be," Washington said. Grandfather marched toward them.

"Gen. Washington, sir," he said, bowing, "I have the pleasure of reporting to you my men's return."

"All safe and sound?"

"We lost four in the harbor skirmish sir, and two to disease. Another two have taken ill since."

"Col. Tims will have our physician see to them straightaway. I hear you've brought powder with you."

"Five kegs, sir. We started with six, but used one to blast our way through the British entrenchments. The Continental Army is also richer by eighteen muskets and twelve bayonets."

"We shall put them to good use," Washington said. "I'm told it was Regina Silsby that found and rescued you."

"Aye, sir, that she did."

"How did she learn of your plight?"

"Blast me to bits if I know, sir. She showed up at my window tonight and . . . well, you see the result."

"Come inside and have a bite of supper with me. I would hear more of your escapade."

"Thank'ee, sir."

"Bye the bye," Washington said, "we haven't seen hide nor hair of your girls since the summer. They went over to Boston after they learned you were lost in the raid."

"Oh, they'll turn up, sir. Quite resourceful, those two. They must be close about."

"I'm sure they are. Well, after we've dined perhaps you should go and find them."

"That I will, sir. Thank'ee, sir."

Washington gazed along the roadway. The hooded figures disappeared over a rise.

"Magnificent," he said.

Twenty

Setbacks

"Hang you for a fool," Cauldon said. "How many prisoners escaped?"

"All of them, sir," Styles said.

"And the deserters?"

"I fear they got off, too, sir."

Cauldon threw his tankard mug across the room.

"Sir," Styles said, "Regina Silsby was in the house before we knew it. I don't see how she managed it."

"Why do you think I posted so many guards about that place?"

"Forgive me, sir, but I don't see why catching her is so important. You said yourself that you intended only to pretend chasing her in order to wreak havoc among the rebels."

"How can I do that when she's in our own barracks stealing our uniforms from us? Today I got the worst tongue lashing since my boyhood."

"I'm sorry, sir."

"She foiled our plot against Washington as easily as falling off a horse. Now she's snatching prisoners from under our very noses. If we don't put an end to her antics soon . . ."

"Why not set a trap for her, sir?"

"Idiot. What did we just do with the Tawney prisoner?"

"Of course, sir. I wasn't thinking."

"I'm beginning to believe Gage is right. Regina Silsby knows our plans before we finish forming them. Her spies must comprise half of Boston's populace."

"With respect, sir, most Bostonians fear her as much as our soldiers. As to the Washington raid, Regina Silsby succeeded only because we weren't expecting her. Next time we shall certainly fare better."

"As we did with the Tawney prisoner?"

"We must impress upon the men a greater sense of urgency."

"She can't be acting alone," Cauldon said. "There may be scores of men masquerading as Regina Silsby."

"Were that so, sir, wouldn't we see her more often?"

"Until we've caught her, we can't be confident of anything. By heaven, I'll see her neck in a noose."

"Where do you think she'll strike next, sir?"

"How am I to know? We'll have to fashion a way to coax her out of hiding—force her hand."

"Sir, why not run skirmishes to the mainland as you originally proposed? I humbly suggest that Gage's ire is just the excuse you need to redouble your efforts."

"And if Regina Silsby shows herself in Boston while we're afield?"

"Leave a handful of the lads here to chase after her. The rest we'll deploy beyond the river. Even if she is only one person acting alone, we can claim there's a whole coven of ghosts besetting us, just as the Sons of Liberty were wont to do."

Slowly Cauldon nodded.

"Perhaps there's something useful in that thick skull of yours after all, Styles."

"Aye, sir."

"If we carry on as planned, we may catch her in the act of resisting us and kill her ourselves."

"One thing is certain, sir: we must be more secretive about our plans."

"There may yet be a card or two we can play. I wish to make the most of them."

Twenty-one

❦

Epiphany

A fire blazed in the stone hearth. Old Farmer Endicott sat nearby, his booted foot rocking a baby cradle, his grizzled hands sifting wool that his wife was spinning into yarn. Rachel stirred the cooking pot while Sarah read aloud the Scriptures.

" 'And lo, the star, which they saw in the east, went before them,' " she read, " 'till it came and stood over where the young child was. When they saw the star, they rejoiced with exceeding great joy.' "

"Mr. Endicott," said his wife, "you should learn to read."

He spat into the flames. The couple had bartered bed and board for the girls' labor during harvest, and Mrs. Endicott was glad of their company. Through the autumn they had busied themselves preserving meats, fruits, and vegetables, making and mending clothes, tending animals, and preparing the farm for winter. As December faded into January, they had much idle time. Sarah devoured the Scriptures as if seeing them for the first time, all the while badgering Rachel with questions.

"Imagine seeing such a star," Sarah said. "It must have been a grand spectacle."

She opened the shutter and gazed into the night. Snow swirled among the evergreens.

"I wonder if the shepherds' hill country looked anything like ours," she said. "Do you suppose it was snowing the night Jesus was born?"

The door rattled. Endicott reached for his rifle.

"Who is it?" Rachel called through the planks.

"Your grandfather, lass. Open up."

She unfastened the latch. Wind and ice billowed through the entry as Grandfather crossed the threshold.

"Saints alive," he said, stamping his feet and stripping off his scarf. " 'Tis a cold night tonight."

" 'Tain't nothing," Endicott said. "Seen far worse."

"What's the word?" Rachel said after securing the door. Grandfather peeled off his coat and hung it on a peg.

"If that's a stew simmering on the hearth there," he said, "I wouldn't mind tasting a bit of it."

"Sit here," Rachel said, offering her stool to him. "I'll pour out some for you."

"We couldn't have lodged you much farther from the rebel camps, now could we?"

"Tell us what news you've brought," she said while handing him a wooden bowl filled to the brim.

"Any bread?"

"Here you are. Now what have you learned of my brother?"

Grandfather spooned meat into his mouth and swallowed a chunk of bread. At last he sighed and said, "There's no sign of him among the militias. Gen. Washington's aides have searched every unit, and I've been through most of them myself. With the new year just come, the army's breaking up. A lot of the men are going home."

"How can they do that?" Rachel said. "The war is hardly won."

"Most of them are through with fighting. A year was all they promised, and the time's about done. This cold weather's not helping matters much"

"What will Gen. Washington do without an army?"

"Raise another if he's up to it."

Endicott scoffed.

"Robert must be returning to Boston, then," Rachel said.

"If he's with the army at all," Grandfather said, "we would know of it."

"He can't have dropped off the face of the earth."

"Perhaps he has, lass."

She stared into the fire. Logs that had once been a robust tree were slowly crumbling to ash. Perhaps her brother, too, was returning to dust.

"What can we do?" she said.

"Sometimes there's not much a body can do," Grandfather said.

"We can't just go home."

"Rachel, don't you suppose your kin are fretting about you and Sarah?"

"We've sent letters."

"Letters don't always get through, lass. More than a month's passed since your last."

"Paper's so hard to come by."

"How is your mother to know that?"

Rachel hung her head.

"The general's been asking after you two," he said. "Looks to me like he misses the both of you."

"We only met with him once," Rachel said, "and even then we never sat down to dinner."

"Still, you've struck a chord on his heartstrings."

She wondered if Washington sat at that same moment before another fire, gazing into its flames, wondering how to replace his disintegrating army. She remembered his words about ordinary people making a mark on events. Six months since his comment he had affected little, and she had affected less.

"Grandfather," she said, "have I been wrong to come here?"

"By my faith, lass. Why do you ask a question like that?"

"We've had no success at all finding Robert."

"You've got to trust the Lord, child. Sometimes we go for one purpose, and God means it for entirely another. You came to Boston expecting to bring home your brother. The Lord had in mind for you to be about another task."

"I'm glad we came," Sarah said, gripping the Bible to her breast.

Rachel smiled and said, "So am I."

Bridles jingled in the stable yard.

"Someone's outside," Endicott said.

"Dismount," said a voice. Endicott rose and peered through the open shutter.

"Lobster backs," he said. "Two wagons plus horsemen."

"Rachel, Sarah, up to the loft with you," Grandfather said. "Stay out of sight."

He squinted into the snowstorm and said, "By my faith, 'tis Maj. Cauldon. Looks like I'll be hiding alongside you lasses. Under the bed, quick now."

A fist hammered the door.

"Open, in the name of the king."

Grandfather mounted the ladder and squeezed under the bed beside the girls. Through a gap beneath the quilt they watched Endicott tug open the door. Cauldon tracked snow into the room.

"We need food and fodder," he said.

"I've nothing to spare you," Endicott said.

"Liar. Get out and see to the horses, or I'll have you shot. You, woman, set a table. I've four-and-twenty stomachs that need filling."

Soldiers spilled through the entry and crowded the room. They were clad in a variety of garments, none of them red. But for Cauldon's presence they might have been mistaken for local militia.

"Look, here's a stew brewing," said one man. He passed a dripping ladle among his comrades, who drained and refilled it until the pot was empty. Endicott's liquor jug was poured into canteens.

"Eat well, men," Cauldon said, "we've a long night ahead of us. I suppose I should make this little jaunt of ours official. Tell me, woman, have you seen Regina Silsby hereabouts?"

"Who?"

"The Boston ghost."

"If she be a Boston ghost, why should she show herself here in Framingham?"

"So she has been seen," Cauldon said. "Where did you say? The hills to the west?"

"I said no such thing."

"I distinctly heard you say, 'The ghost terrorized my husband and me and then fled westward into the hill country.' Tell me, Styles, did I hear her aright?"

"Close enough, sir."

" 'Tis settled, then," Cauldon said. "My superiors have ordered me to chase Regina Silsby and chase her I shall to the ends of the earth, if necessary. Ho, men, I say we have a look westward. Who knows but we may catch the wench in some dastardly wickedness. And if we happen to run across anything else, well . . . we'll have to wait and see."

The men laughed.

"Something's afoot," Rachel whispered.

"Plain as the nose on your face," Grandfather said.

From beneath the bed frame they watched the soldiers empty the larder of flour, meal, dried fruits, salted meat, and eggs. One soldier pocketed the wool Mrs. Endicott had spun; another took the rifle from the hearth. Candles, brass, and linen were all squirreled into pockets and pouches. Two men climbed the loft and circled the bed, knocking things about but finding nothing of interest. They descended the ladder empty-handed.

"Madame, we shall be back with the dawn," Cauldon said. "Pray be ready with another meal for us. Fail and I shall burn down your dwelling. But don't fret. It shan't be a great loss to any but your vermin. Fall out, men. To the wagons with you."

The soldiers clambered outside, leaving the rooms in shambles. Shouted commands sent the wagons rattling through the gate.

"Cursed thieves," Endicott said as he banged shut the door. His wife began to sob.

"Come along, children, we've no time to waste," Grandfather said. "Endicott, have you a pair of horses?"

"Four in the barn. Why?"

"We're following after the redcoats."

"You're daft, man. Them wagons is loaded with grenades. Saw them myself as I was foddering the horses. They're expecting to fight an army."

"Perhaps we may give warning. Who knows, you may come out richer by two wagons and several horses. We'll save your dwelling, at any rate. What say you?"

"I'll come along and make sure of it."

"Thank'ee kindly, sir, but your wife needs tending, and we can manage by ourselves. We've done this sort of thing afore."

Endicott scratched his head, nodded, and ventured outside.

"Load your pistols, lasses," Grandfather said. "Rachel, see what you can find for knives in the kitchen. And dress warmly, both of you. 'Twill be a busy night."

After gathering their sundries, the girls bundled themselves in multiple layers of wool and tramped outside.

Endicott had three horses saddled at the barn. Amidst hurried good byes the girls galloped with Grandfather through the falling snow, their breath icing before them, their cheeks stinging from the cold. Over hills and valleys they rode, tracing the wagons' tracks into the wooded heights beyond Framingham.

"Hold," Grandfather said, reining to a halt. "The redcoats stopped at this clearing here."

He dismounted and studied the marks in the snow.

"Some of them have ventured off on foot," he said. "See those boot trails in the snow yonder? Four or five of them, I'd say."

"A scouting party?" Rachel said.

"They're lugging a lot of stuff with them," he said. "The snow beneath their feet is packed hard."

"Mr. Endicott told us they were carrying grenades."

"Let's follow after this little detachment and see where they take us."

"But if the main body is still forging ahead . . ."

"We'll need more weapons than we've got to harass them," he said. "Along this path we'll find five lads packing grenades, and they'll be wandering all alone in a forest haunted by ghosts. Now my thinking is, if Regina Silsby throws grenades as well as she throws knives . . ."

"Let us follow after the scouts."

"On with your faces first."

The girls masked and gloved themselves. Grandfather produced a tattered hide of his own and covered his head with it.

"I thought I might be needing a new one," he said while clamping his tricornered hat over his bald scalp, "since Sarah's taken a fancy to mine. And this mask doesn't smell at all bad."

"Corpses are supposed to make a stench," Sarah said. "You can hardly consider yourself a proper ghoul if you're not foul-scented."

"My ghost will have to be freshly dead," he said, remounting. "Come along; let's be off."

They descended a slippery slope and crossed a frozen stream. On the next ridge they spotted four men trudging through the snow. Muskets were slung over their shoulders, and heavy rucksacks bent their backs. They disappeared over the rise.

"Rachel," Grandfather said, "circle atop that ridge there, and we'll trap them in the gully. Give us an owl's hoot when you're in position. Sing something as they're approaching you. Let them know you're a woman. 'Twill drop their guard. We'll surprise them from behind."

"And if they should attack me?"

"Chances are good their muskets will be unloaded, to avoid an accidental discharge. Surprise is their game, lass. All we need do is spoil it. Besides, you'll escape them easily enough. They're weighted down with heavy loads, and you're astride a horse. But have your pistol ready, just the same."

She peeled away from the pair and circled her mount through the trees. At a copse of snowy pines she spied the men climbing toward her, cursing as they lost their footing, grasping rocks and mounds of earth to halt their tumbling. She mimicked an owl's hoot and heard a distant reply.

"Move along, you laggards," said the leader, "we're almost at the crest. Another mile or two and . . ."

He halted.

"Look there," he said, "who's that atop the ridge?"

Rachel had eased her horse from the shadows and was singing to herself.

"Lord, who through these forty days
For us didst fast and pray,
Teach us with Thee to mourn our sins
And close by Thee to stay."

"I say, woman, who are you?" said the soldier. He climbed toward her. "How's a woman come to be out in this wilderness so late? Lost, are you?"

She continued humming her tune, her face hidden in her cloak.

"Speak up, lass, what's your name?" he said, approaching her and reaching for her horse's bridle. "What's brought you so far afield?"

She turned on him.

"You have," she said, in her toad's voice. He yelped and staggered backward. With her pistol she whacked his skull and sent him tumbling down the slope.

"God save us," said another, " 'Tis Regina Silsby."

Two mounted banshees fell shrieking on the remaining men. Hammer blows silenced their screams. Grandfather dismounted and stripped the soldiers of their weapons, pouches, and packs.

"They'll wake up afore long," he said, "and by then we must be gone. Now, what have we here?"

He tore open a rucksack and rummaged through its contents.

"Grenades," he said, lifting one of the iron balls from the pack, "eight of them, already fused. Rachel, Sarah, dump out the sacks of everything but the bombs. Each of you hang a bag on your saddle, and we'll divide the grenades among us."

"Look here," Sarah said, " 'tis Mr. Endicott's rifle."

"He'll be glad to have it back. Come along."

They retraced their steps and were soon following the rutted tracks of the wagons. Gunshots boomed in the forest ahead.

"Hurry on," Grandfather said, urging his horse forward. In the next gully they found two wagons untended.

"They're not expecting any trouble from their rear, that's clear enough," he said, slipping from his saddle. After un-hitching the wagon's horses, he slapped the animals' flanks and sent them galloping toward Framingham.

"Bring the muskets and the cartridge pouches," he said, remounting. They ascended the hill and saw flashes bright-ening the valley beyond. Sizzling grenades arced toward a frozen stream, where a handful of guns blasted in reply.

"Whoever they are, the redcoats have got them trapped," Grandfather said. "Let's see if we can stir things up a bit. We'll tether the horses yonder out of sight. Rachel, take a musket and get you to the left flank there. Load up and wait for my signal. Sarah, you do the same to the right. When you see my bomb fall among them, light your fuses with your pistol flints and throw. Once that's done, shoot your musket, then change your position five or ten yards. Reload, throw and fire again. Got it?"

They nodded.

"Don't fret yourself with accuracy," he said, "we just want to appear more than we are. With luck we'll scare them off. Each of you throw only four grenades, then meet back here. We'll decide then how we progress."

"Aye, Captain," Sarah said, hoisting a musket to her shoulder and disappearing to the right. Rachel grabbed a gun and slithered along the opposite ridge. At a frosted boulder she paused to prime and load. Soldiers below fired toward the stream and hurled bombs that exploded near its banks. Farther along a detachment moved to flank the creek's defenders.

She ran along the crest, hoping to outdistance them. A fallen limb tripped her. Down the slope she skidded in a cloud of tumbling snow. Her arms wrapped a tree, halting her slide. From atop the ridge Grandfather's bomb sailed into the valley. A second grenade followed after it and bounced down the hill. Frantically Rachel searched for her musket. It lay among the boulders farther down. She slid toward it, fending rocks with her hands and feet. Grandfather's bomb erupted, and Sarah's exploded immediately after. Two musket shots boomed from the heights.

Rachel tore off her pack and dug out a grenade. She pressed her pistol's firelock to the fuse and pointed the gun down the slope. With a flash and a bang the pistol discharged, sparking the cord. She hurled the orb as far as she could. Its fiery tail descended through the trees and vanished.

"Mercy," she said, realizing it had sputtered out. She rummaged through her pack for a second grenade when the missile blasted among the pines. Relieved, she grabbed her musket and stumbled several yards before remembering to fire it. A jerk of the trigger sent a lead ball screaming down the slope. With the long gun's firelock she ignited a second grenade and threw that as well. Its fireball drove soldiers from their cover. More grenades rained from Grandfather's and Sarah's positions, followed by musket fire. Hurrahs sounded behind the stream, and armed men rushed across the banks.

The soldiers retreated toward her. She scrambled up the slope, scattering snow and grit. Her boot slipped, and she tumbled in an avalanche of stone and ice. Rocks tore away her pack and ripped the musket from her grip. She spilled toward the stream, clawing for a handhold and finally latching onto a stone that tore her skin. Despite the agony she clung to the granite and halted her plummet. A lone grenade lay in the snow beside her. With a bloody hand she seized it, her fingers staining the frost, and snapped the pistol flint against the fuse. Sparks flared and she pitched the bomb downhill. The blast illuminated a band running toward her. Two fell. She struggled over a granite outcrop. Her foot sank into a crag, and her ankle wrenched. Pain speared her leg. She collapsed, and the soldiers stampeded past her. One man halted. It was Maj. Cauldon.

"Regina Silsby," he said. "The devil take you."

He pressed a pistol to her brow and pulled the trigger. The pan sparked, but no shot erupted.

"Hang your filthy carcass," he said, casting aside the gun and reaching for his sword. Musket balls splintered the trees around him. A shot mangled the hilt of his blade. He cried out and stumbled away, cursing and clutching his hand. Rachel struggled to her feet, but the agony in her ankle pitched her to her knees. A mounted man drew rein before her, a sword dangling at his side and a rifle perched on his thigh. He gasped and leveled his gun. With a shriek she hurled herself to the ground. The rifle discharged. Behind her stood a soldier poised to thrust a bayonet into her back. The horseman's bullet holed his breast, and he dropped into a snowdrift.

"God have mercy," said the horseman. He leapt from his mount, knelt over her, and turned her on her back. She blinked into the disbelieving face of her brother.

"Robert," she said.

"By my faith," he said. "Rachel, I can hardly believe it. What in heaven's name are you doing here?"

"You're armed like a bandit."

"And you're ghastly," he said. " 'Tis true then, you are the ghost. I suspected it, but . . ."

"You haven't told anyone, have you?"

"Not a soul. But how do you come to be here?"

"Searching for you," she said, "to bring you out of Boston."

"You think me unable to care for myself? I've managed well enough."

"But where have you been?"

"Fetching the Ticonderoga guns. We're bringing them up now."

"Where are they?"

"Half a league behind. We heard the ruckus and guessed that our scouts were in trouble. Some of us came along to help out. You're not out here alone, are you?"

"Grandfather's atop the bluff, with—"

"You there," said a gruff voice. A buckskinned marauder halted his horse beside them. Fur crowned his bearded face, and leather fringed his stout arms. The muzzle of his long rifle stretched toward them.

"Robert, lad," he said. "Saints alive, man, I almost shot you. Who is this hag you've got your arms about?"

"She's my . . . I mean to say, she's . . . she's the ghost, sir. Regina Silsby."

"Regina Silsby? No wonder them redcoats have flown the coop."

Rachel gripped Robert's lapel.

"I've hurt my ankle," she said into his ear. "I can't walk."

"Miss Regina Silsby," he said with a cough, "I don't suppose you'd care to accompany us back to our regiment. I'd be most honored if you'd ride my horse."

"Take me up the ridge," she said in her frog's voice. "That is all I require of you."

"With your permission, sir," Robert said to the horseman.

"Aye, wherever she wishes," he said and urged his mount back toward the stream. "I'll not dispute the desires of a ghost, especially one who chases away the king's men."

Robert lifted Rachel into his saddle.

"Better?" he said.

"Grandfather's atop the hill there," she said, "but beware. He's got grenades and muskets."

"Where did he get them?"

"From the soldiers attacking you. We overran a detachment on your flank."

"Incredible."

"Who goes there?" said a voice from the trees on the hillcrest.

"Robert Winslow. I'm fetching up Regina Silsby to you."

"How's that again?"

"I'm Robert Winslow of Col. Knox's regiment. Regina Silsby's with me."

"Is she? Speak up, lass, let me hear you."

"I am here," Rachel said.

"By my faith, come along then, both of you."

Robert led his horse up the rise.

"Saints alive," Grandfather said, throwing his arms around his grandson. "It is you, Robert, sure enough. We've spent months searching after you."

"Good heavens," Robert said, "you're a ghost too, are you, Grandfather? And who's this with you?"

"Your cousin Sarah."

"Sarah Gooding? You can't mean that."

" 'Tis true enough," she said, still gripping a musket in her fists.

"When last we met," Robert said, "you were but a skinny rail."

"I've grown since."

"And died and gone to perdition as well by the look of you. Come along back to the camp with me, all of you. We've much to talk about."

"I fear you must come to us," Rachel said.

"Why?"

"We cannot risk anyone learning who we are."

"I shan't be able to leave the colonel until the guns are delivered. There's fifty of them, Rachel, plus mortars. All the way from Lake Champlain we've brought them."

"We're lodged in Framingham," she said, "at the Endicott farm. You'll pass directly by."

"The colonel may allow me some time," he said. "I've become a right hand to him, Rachel."

"Robert, lad, is that you?" called a voice from the stream.

"There's the colonel now," he said. "Come and meet him."

"It appears the colonel is coming to meet us."

Torches ascended the ridge. In their glow marched a rotund, hatless man with bronze curls teasing his brow and pink jowls shaking at every step. He was uniformed in buff and blue with a lined cape draping his shoulders. Despite his bulk he bounced up the hill with more energy than all the men surrounding him.

"Too much light they're bringing," Grandfather said. "Come, children, we shouldn't be seen. Robert, get your sister on her own horse and gather up these muskets for your men. We'll await you at the Endicott farm. Time enough to talk then."

"Aye, sir. I'll very much look forward to it."

"And we. Come along, lasses."

"You go ahead," Rachel said. "I wish to greet the colonel."

"I shall stay as well," Sarah said.

"Suit yourselves, but don't tarry long. I'll await you by the wagons."

The girls were saddled on their own horses when Knox reached the summit.

"Well met, son," he said, shaking Robert's hand. "What's this I hear of Regina Silsby?"

"She's here, sir," Robert said.

"Upon my word, so she is. Regina Silsby, I'm told you have spared my men a nasty drubbing. For that I thank you most sincerely."

"The dawn approaches, Colonel," she said in her toad's voice. "My sister and I must be back to our graves."

"You've a sister? Good heavens, so you have. I was hoping you'd stay to breakfast and tell me how you managed it."

"Ghosts do not eat."

"No, I suppose not. Well, if you must depart, I shan't stop you. Go with God, Regina Silsby. And you, too, Miss . . . Miss . . ."

"Rebecca," Sarah said.

"Miss Rebecca. Regina and Rebecca Silsby, is it? Very well, then, my thanks to you both."

"Greet Gen. Washington for us," Rachel said, "when you deliver your guns to him."

"So I shall. Will he be surprised to learn that we have met?"

"Perhaps not."

The girls reined their horses down the slope. Knox stood watching until they vanished.

"Would to God we had a hundred such as they," he said.

Twenty-two

On Dorchester Heights

Gen. Washington surveyed the gun emplacements on the bluff. Dusk darkened Boston harbor, and gale winds laced with freezing rain lashed the hill. January had seen his worst fears realized. In less than a fortnight the Continental Army had dwindled from twenty-five thousand to less than three. But like Joshua's warriors of old, the remnant had proven themselves hardy souls. In a single night they had occupied Dorchester Heights and dragged the Ticonderoga guns to the summit. Timber walls were erected and trees felled to form an impenetrable tangle around the fort. In the center of their stockade stood a tall liberty pole, and the colonials' striped banner whipped at its crown.

"A glorious sight," Knox said above the tempest. "From here the mighty British Navy is nothing but toy boats bobbing in a bath. We'll put them to flight or send every one of them to the bottom."

"Most impressive," Washington said. "You've done us a great service, Colonel."

"When may we commence the bombardment, sir?"

"God willing, never."

"Sir?"

"This afternoon I received a parley from the citizens of Boston. They carried with them a British promise not to burn the town if we allow their fleet to retire unmolested."

"Gen. Washington, sir, I say we let loose on them—show them what we can do."

"They know it too well, Colonel. Our hope is to win our liberties, not to kill our fellow men."

"Sir, if we don't destroy them, they'll be back to fight us another day. I say we put an end to them here and now. With some heated shot we could set the bigger ships ablaze and sink one or two in the channel mouth there. That would trap every last one of them in the harbor. They'd be forced to surrender or sink. Within a fortnight we could be commissioning the whole fleet into the Continental Navy."

"What would become of the civilians, Colonel?"

"Sir?"

"Those ships are packed stem to stern with your Boston neighbors."

"They're Tories, sir, loyal to the crown, not to us."

"Even so, if we fire on the ships, we may kill many innocents and see all Boston burned before our eyes."

"Once the redcoats see their position is hopeless—"

"Desperate men do desperate things, Colonel. Suppose we trap the fleet as you propose, and still they refuse to surrender?"

"We'd be forced to batter them into submission. But such a course would be suicidal."

"And if they burn the city? How many civilians might die in the blaze?"

"A great many, I suppose."

"Indeed."

Washington pressed a hand to his hat and strolled the parapet.

"I'm told," he said, "that in Great Britain there is much sympathy for our cause. If we make Boston a bloodbath, we may lose that sympathy and see ourselves assailed by fleets and armies ten times larger. Can you foresee such a possibility?"

"An infuriated people can be a formidable opponent, sir."

"Lexington and Concord proved as much. Tell me, Colonel, what is your estimation of our chances against a determined, wrathful enemy ten times our size?"

"In truth, sir, I would have to say—"

"Poor? I agree. Therefore, I am inclined to accept Gen. Howe's proposal and allow the fleet to retire."

Knox sighed. For months he had anticipated watching the British ships burn.

"Don't think your effort's been wasted," Washington said. "It is only from our present position of strength, given us by you, that we may be merciful. Our kindness today will shout to all Britain that our intentions are benevolent. Who knows? Perhaps we may win our liberties without further conflict."

"And if you're mistaken, sir?"

"That depends on King George. As for me, I would rather err on the side of right and mercy."

Knox scanned the bay and stifled a chuckle.

"Something amuses you, Colonel?"

"Begging your pardon, sir, but it seems odd that such benevolence should come from one who's made arms his profession."

"The purpose of arms," Washington said, "is to be so mighty with them that they are never needed. Unless we possess great strength in this sinful world, we shall never know peace."

Together they watched the winds hammer the harbor. Warships tugged at their anchor chains, and waves battered the shoreline. Ice and snow swirled across the seas and scourged the hillsides. On a crest to the east winked a single lantern.

"Look, sir," Knox said, "there she is again."

Washington stretched his spyglass toward the bluff. Through the gale he discerned two hooded figures atop the crag, one clutching a lantern. Cloaks and skirts billowed as the pair gazed across the harbor. Washington kept his glass trained on them until one turned toward the fort. Her face was rotted wreckage.

"So she is," Washington said. "Once more Regina Silsby has blessed us by her presence."

"The men say she brought the tempest upon us," Knox said.

"And God bless her for it, Colonel. The storm has prevented a British attack before our fort was finished. Be she a ghost or not, she has been a covering angel to us."

"I daresay she has the Lord's favor, sir. Whenever she appears, our cause prospers."

"So it would seem."

To himself Washington said, "And who can measure the contributions of a single man or woman?"

"Begging your pardon, sir?"

"Nothing, Colonel. I was recalling something I once said to a young lady."

Rachel stood with Sarah on the hilltop, her lantern swinging in her hand.

"Strange, is it not?" Sarah said, her voice muffled by her mask. "Night after night we stand here praying for peace, and all the while people in Boston do the same. But we pray for a patriot victory, and they pray for a redcoat victory. Our visions of a proper peace differ so greatly that we are at each other's throats over it."

"Only God knows the end of all of this," Rachel said.

"I wish He would show us. Then we might pray aright."

"If He spoke that plainly, we would never need faith."

"Why does faith seem everything to Him? He never shines so brightly that we can act with any confidence."

"It would save us all a lot of trouble," Rachel said. "But instead we must pray by the light He gives us and follow Him as best we can."

"Which means we blunder through our days hoping to bear good fruit by them. It seems most inefficient to me. Father in heaven, can you not brighten Your lantern a bit for us? If You have any regard at all for Rachel and me, do show us some reason for this misery."

She stood in silence, watching the ships heave on the churning waters. Masts and yardarms swayed in the tempest, streaming ice and spray.

"It is dark," she said at last, and turned toward the path descending the hill.

"Has He answered you?" Rachel said.

"No, but I shan't give up asking. Perhaps He will think me serious if I pester Him enough. But just now the soup will be boiling, and Grandfather will have news from the rebel camps. Are you coming?"

"I shall be along presently."

"Don't tarry too long. You'll catch your death in this tempest."

"I rather like it."

Sarah descended the bluff, and Rachel gazed back across the harbor. Dimly lit windows in the town faded behind sheets of snow. Roiling clouds blackened the heavens. She clutched her hood more tightly to her chin.

"Marvelous view from here," said a stranger. Rachel spun around. Maj. Cauldon stood on the fringe of the bluff, his tunic's crimson tails flapping behind him. A pistol was tucked into his waistband, and a sword dangled from his sash.

"Regina Silsby," he said, stepping toward her, "there's not a man, woman, or child in all Boston who hasn't seen you atop this bluff. What are you about, we all wonder? Casting some wicked spell upon us?"

She backed away from him.

"Afraid of me, are you?" he said, drawing his sword. "But how can that be? What ghost fears a mortal? And how is it that my sudden appearance seems to have caught you off-guard? You know how easily the rebel pickets are avoided, especially in such wild weather as this. By the by, you'll be glad to hear that Gen. Howe has ordered Boston evacuated as soon as the storm lifts. It seems you've won, Regina Silsby. That should bring you some satisfaction. But we've unfinished business, you and I. Let us talk, shall we? Face-to-face and man-to-man? Take off that mask."

"What mask?" she said in her frog's voice.

"Don't think me such a simpleton," he said. "Cowards and fools you may dupe by your antics. Remove your mask at once. I would see your face."

"No."

"Strip it off, you beggar's bride, or I shall run you through."

"You intend to do that anyway. If you would see my face, 'twill be dead when you gaze upon it. I'll not yield while I live."

Slowly they circled each other, separated by the gleaming blade.

"Your rebel bravado is wasted on me, Regina Silsby," he said. "Satisfaction shall be mine."

With his free hand he grabbed at her throat. She swatted aside his arm and bashed the lamp against his brow.

"Filthy, wretched peasant," he said, nursing a gash on his forehead. "I'll have your hide for that."

258

He lunged at her. She dodged the blade and swung the lantern at his temple. Glass shattered. The blow sent him staggering, and she bolted down the slope toward the trees.

"You shan't escape me, Regina Silsby," he said. "I'll hunt you down like a dog."

At a cluster of elms she halted, panting. Somehow her wick still burned. The lantern was her only weapon, yet its light betrayed her position. She shook its brass belly. Too little oil remained to start a fire. Could she douse the major and set him ablaze? Unlikely.

"Lord, help me," she said. Already Cauldon's footfalls tramped toward her. She decided her flame was useless. The hurricane globe's jagged edges might serve as a weapon, but they would be no match for Cauldon's sharpened steel. Her fingers were poised to snuff the wick when a better idea struck her.

On a stub of broken branch she hung the lamp and scurried behind a nearby tree. Rocks scattered at her feet. She grabbed two and clutched them in her fists.

"I have you now," Cauldon said, leaping past the tree and striking at the lantern. His sword buried itself in the trunk. She burst from her shelter and bludgeoned his skull with her stones. He reeled backward, and the blade wrenched free. Into a pine thicket she melted.

"You sow's whelp," he said, flailing his sword and stumbling on the steep ground. Shadows pranced across the trees as the flame pitched in the wind. He tore the lantern loose and flung it to the earth. The flame sputtered and died.

"Come out, Regina Silsby," he said. "Your end will be all the worse if you resist me."

Aye, make your noise, she thought. Sarah and Grandfather would hear and come to her aid. Or would they? The howling tempest smothered every sound. Unless she lured him closer to the cottage, no one would know her peril.

From the frost at her feet she pried a piece of timber and pitched it down the slope. The stick tumbled through the trees, scattering snow. Cauldon bolted after it, then halted. Slowly he surveyed the rise above him.

"Your silly ruses do not fool me, Regina Silsby," he said. "By heaven, I shall find you."

She peeled off her cloak and draped it on a rotted trunk jutting from the ground. Wind spilled through the woolen folds as she knotted tight the collar's cord. Cauldon spotted the movement and climbed toward her. Using the cape to shield herself from his sight, she drifted to the fringe of the thicket and left her effigy alone among the evergreens. Once free of the pines, she fled into the forest.

"Die, Regina Silsby," Cauldon shouted. His sword hacked the wooden figure, and moments later his rage rebounded through the woods. Rachel quickened her pace. Lightning brightened the trees before her, and thunder echoed at her back. A musket ball whistled past her head. Perhaps he had seen her wig billowing across her back. She stripped off the hairpiece and impaled it on a stick.

Patches of snow before her traversed a rocky overhang. Its granite wall plummeted twenty feet to a slab of rock. Could she force Cauldon over it? Frantically she scanned her surroundings and spied a limb fallen from an oak. She scooped up the branch and darted behind a tree. When Cauldon appeared, she would batter him over the precipice.

Gusts tousled her skirts and tangled the leather cords dangling at her neck. Vainly she struggled to control the shudders rattling her jaw and limbs. Tortured heartbeats hammered her chest, and frigid air speared her lungs. She adjusted her grip on the bludgeon and eyed the cliff's approach.

A blow to the back of her skull pitched her to the frozen earth.

"You stupid hag," Cauldon said, standing over her. "Thought to trick me again, did you? What a shame you couldn't keep the wind from ruffling your dress. I saw it behind the tree there."

He kicked her ribs and sent her tumbling.

"Don't expect to die quickly," he said. "I shall beat you within an inch of your life until your bruised and bloody carcass crawls before me pleading for mercy. A thousand cuts I'll make in your flesh and relish every howl you make. Before I've done, you will beg me to kill you. And I shan't do it, do you hear? I'll slit your throat when I am ready, not when you wish it. You'll die admitting you are wretched scum."

She struggled to raise herself.

"What's the matter, witch?" he said. "Can you not make some devilish magic and fly away, or curse me with a foul disease? Why not conjure up fires from hell and burn me to ash? Forgotten the spell, have you? Perhaps this will jog your memory."

He kicked her again. The blow left her gasping.

"You are dirt under my soles, Regina Silsby," he said, "mud I scrape from my boots. You're not fit for pigs to trample upon, not worth a proper grave. I shall cut up your corpse and hang its pieces on the town gates. The ravens and crows will pick apart your rotting flesh."

With his boot he forced her on her back and pressed the tip of his sword to her belly.

"Wounds to the bowels are the worst," he said. "They rarely kill straightaway, but they are excruciating. I wonder how many you can survive. But let us see first how much more ugly you are than that ridiculous mask you wear. Remove it."

"No."

His sharpened steel pierced her dress.

"I will see your face," he said, twisting the blade.

"Not before I'm dead."

"I shall persuade you differently."

"If you kill me, you may wish you had not."

"Don't test my patience with riddles. You cannot be the person I suspect."

"And if I am?"

"Impossible."

"So certain are you, Major?"

"Scoundrel. You'll lose your tongue for that. I'll not be made a fool, by you or anyone else. And don't fret for your sister, or whatever it is you call your companion. I'll deal with her after I've done with you."

A shot rang out. Cauldon staggered. Something had struck his back. At the same moment his chest seemed scalded by a firebrand. He stared at his tunic and discovered a fresh hole oozing blood. Dizziness spun his brow. Through the trees drifted a second phantom, her milky face surrounded by golden tresses that streamed like ribbons on the wind. Luminous fabric billowed from her shoulders and her waist. In her outstretched hand she clutched a smoldering pistol.

"You," he said, stepping toward her. "It can't be. You're . . . you're . . ."

His legs buckled. The sword dropped from his grasp. He toppled and lay groaning on the ground.

The golden phantom approached his fallen form.

"I know you," Cauldon said. "The night of the comedy . . ."

Regina Silsby appeared at her side, her skull shorn of its tangled locks.

"And you," he said, "you must be . . . but that's impossible . . . you're . . . not . . ."

His head dropped back.

"Two sisters," he said, coughing, "one dark, the other fair . . ."

His eyes glazed, and his chest stopped heaving.

"Sarah," Rachel said, "you've killed him."

"I saved you."

Twenty-three

❧

Evacuation

Fifes and drums trailed the colonials' flag through Boston Gate. Church bells clattered, trumpets blared, and guns thundered as the rebel army filed beneath the bricked arch. The cobbled lanes were crowded with cheering throngs. Onlookers in the windows waved handkerchiefs and banged cooking pots.

"Let me be the first to welcome you home, Col. Knox," Washington said above the din.

"Thank you very much indeed, sir," Knox said. He rode at Washington's side, a fist planted on one hip, a gloved hand clutching his reins. Robert followed among his mounted companions. Behind them marched the rebel army through entrenchments strewn with slaughtered animals, wrecked wagons, and mangled gun carriages.

"We may be able to salvage some of it, General," Knox said.

"As soon as we've secured the town," Washington said. "Just now we've many people who wish to greet us."

Among the army's ranks swarmed crowds of refugees: merchants, masons, milliners, cobblers, carpenters, printers, tailors, seamen, women, children. They towed carts, pushed barrows, drove wagons, all the while staring at the dilapidated city they had once called home. Trees were gone, churches stripped, shops and dwellings razed.

An explosion boomed across the harbor. Castle Island's fortress collapsed into smoking wreckage, and the British bombardiers who had blasted it retreated to their longboats. In the channel a frigate waited with the rest of the British fleet to carry them home to England.

"They haven't left us much of anything," Knox said.

"We have the town," Washington said, "and we have our liberty. For now we shall content ourselves with that."

Atop Dorchester's distant height he spied two cloaked women surveying the town.

"See there, Colonel," he said, nodding toward the hill. "Yonder stands the patron saint of Boston."

"A grand spectacle," Rachel said, surveying the human flood that poured across Boston Neck.

"Very nice," Grandfather said. "Something to write home about. Now come along, children, our chores here are done. Time we headed back to Philadelphia."

"Indeed," Sarah said. "If we tarry much longer, my mother shall begin to fret."

"She's got nothing to fear where you're concerned," he said. "I'd be more anxious for the regiments coming against you."

Sarah scanned the city a final time and sighed.

"Why so glum?" Rachel said. "We're homeward bound at last."

"I suppose your family will be returning to Boston," she said, "now that the port's liberated."

"Mercy, I hadn't thought of that," Rachel said. "I expect my father shan't see any reason to remain in Philadelphia."

"And just when our merriment's beginning."

"Beginning?"

"Surely you can't expect Regina Silsby to retire now, Rachel. There's too much work ahead."

"But the British are fleeing, Sarah. You can see their ships retreating from here."

"One colony they've abandoned. But mark me well, Rachel Winslow, those redcoats will be back, and in greater numbers. Before long we must see Regina Silsby again, if not in Boston, then in New York or Philadelphia, perhaps even Baltimore or Williamsburg. I'll wager my life on it."

"Already we've risked our lives enough," Rachel said. "I want to go home for a bath and a decent meal. Grandfather, do talk some sense into her."

The old man stuffed tobacco into his pipe.

"She's right about the redcoats, lass," he said. "We'll see more of them afore long, I expect. But can Regina Silsby really do much to stop them? That's another matter."

Sarah sniffed.

"Ye of little faith," she said.